NAHARA

Book 2 of the
Non-Compliant Space Series

S. Verity Reynolds

Weird Books for Weird People

NAHARA, Copyright 2021 Autonomous Press, LLC (Fort Worth, TX, 76114).

Autonomous Press is an independent publisher focusing on works about neurodivergence, queerness, and the various ways they can intersect with each other and with other aspects of identity and lived experience. We are a partnership including writers, poets, artists, musicians, community scholars, and professors. Each partner takes on a share of the work of managing the press and production, and all of our workers are co-owners.

ISBN: 978-1-945955-22-8

Cover art by Nick Walker,
from a photo by Alberto Restifo

Also by Verity Reynolds:
Nantais
(Book 1 of the Non-Compliant Space Series)

to Alexia
be who you are

A Brief Guide to Niralan Grammar

by Koa Nantais, Office of the Ambassador

The basic unit of meaning in Niralanes is the verb. Nearly all words in Niralanes derive from a "root" verb form. Verbs are identifiable primarily by their lack of any grammatical ending, or by the *-ya* (imperative) ending. They also operate as proper names.

Other parts of speech may be identified with the following endings:

-ne	adjective	*-es*	adverb or adjective; "in the manner of"
-ie	proper noun (titles)	*-ya*	proper noun (names)
-pa	noun (things, ideas)	*-ron*	noun (places, events)

Sentences in Niralanes typically appear in subject-object-verb (SOV) order, although in some cases the object precedes the subject for emphasis (similar to the "passive voice" in Earth Standard). Endings that serve grammatical functions include:

-da	possessive	-eya	indirect object/ object of the preposition
-ve	plural (mass; living things)	-vo	plural (discrete; things that can be owned)
-ai	subject. When no verb appears, -ai functions as a copula.		

No contractions are made when adding endings to a word. For instance, if a word ends in *a*, -ai is added directly, without omitting either *a*.

Ina	*doripa*	*an.*
She	(the) book	writes.
Inaai	*anie.*	
She (is) (a)	writer.	
Ina	*doripavo*	*an.*
She	(the) books	write.

Emphasis on indirect objects is indicated by their placement in the sentence; the closer they appear to the subject, the greater the emphasis.

Inaai	*doripa*	*iaeya*	*mai.*
She	(the) book	to you-all	gave. (She gave *the book* to you all.)
Inaai	*iaeya*	*doripa*	*mai.*
She	to you-all	(the) book	gave. (*To you all*, she gave the book.)

Pronouns in Niralanes differ somewhat from those in Alash Kan or Earth Standard. Many speakers of these languages, feeling themselves unable to communicate without certain pronouns, have been known to insert Alash Kan pronouns. This is not recommended unless you know where Aristotle may stuff his triangle. Proper Niralanes pronouns include:

Inae	3d person plural		
Ina	3d person singular polite	*Ilik*	3d person singular inferior
Ia	2d person plural		
Issh	1st person plural mass (we all)	*Ila*	1st person plural discrete (we few)
Ihi	1st person singular (used only when referring to kiiste)		

Niralanes has no first person singular comparable to the Earth Standard *I* or second person singular comparable to the Earth Standard *you*. Many Niralans who have learned Earth Standard have learned to deploy these pronouns in contexts that sound native to an

Earth Standard speaker. It should not, however, be assumed that because a Niralan uses I, she has the same internal experience of individuality as a human.

A non-Niralan speaker should never use *issh* or *ihi*.

Several nouns in Niralanes are irregular. Handle these with care. They invariably indicate a person, place, object, or idea of significant cultural importance.

Nel mezzo del cammin di nostra vita
mi ritrovai per una selva oscura,
ché la diritta via era smarrita.

Dante, Inferno, Canto I

Erin Lang
Personal Log

So I'm a corporate sellout now.

Joking! They couldn't pay me enough. I am on the ISS *Jemison, though, with Cordry. I'm not on the payroll, but that doesn't seem to bother anyone here. I guess when you're out in unregistered space in a ship that should have been mothballed a decade ago, you take whoever you can get.*

But since I'm not on the payroll, I'm probably not on the manifest, either. So we'd better not crash or no one will come looking for my body.

Certainly no one will come looking for this journal, but that's kind of the point. And to think my dads said cryptography was a waste of my talents.

I ran into Cordry again in the Reefer, on Reven. C. got picked up by the Jemison while trying to fix one of our ships, but they seem to think we're all some kind of pirates. Which I guess isn't totally untrue?

Anyway, the Jemison's captain turned out to be David's mom. Her name is Resa — Resa Molloy. She's out here looking for David instead of doing science or what-

ever Interstellar Science thinks you can do on an R1. Answer: Basically nothing. This ship is ancient.

Only David is doing this whole deep cover thing on the Terminus (that creepy prison station that's run by Viidans but owned by the UGR), so he couldn't get rescued like his mom planned.

Instead David and Mom talked Captain Molloy into finding the source of the slave trade on the Terminus — I mean, where all the slaves are coming from. And then Mom told me to get on Molloy's ship, no matter what.

Well, that part was easy. C's had a crush on me for months. And let's face it, I missed the distraction. C's good company, if you don't mind being fawned over in between go-rounds.

The hard part is what Mom told me to do next.

I call Jiya Nantais "Mom," but she's not my mom. She's Dar's mom. Dar is the Jemison's computational linguist (which makes her my "supervisor," ha!). She is, of course, Niralan — I'm pretty sure they can't breed with other species, even if they wanted to.

Dar Nantais is nothing like her mom, though. Jiya understands people, for all she pretends not to like them. Dar is… weird.

Weird for a Niralan, I mean.

It's not just me. Most of the crew finds her even weirder than I do. That's because most of them have never even met a Niralan before, so they're dealing with that and with the fact that Dar herself is creepy. To most of them. The XO here, Commander Hayek, doesn't seem to find her creepy at all, and that's providing good cover. No one wants to gossip about me and C. when they've got Dar and Hayek to gossip about.

He's in love with her. He tries to make like he's this grouchy untouchable fortress, but he looks at her and just melts. It'd be cute if he were in any way attractive himself.

Rumor is they're sleeping together, but what she thinks of him, no one has any idea, because of course she doesn't even respond to questions about it, just looks at you like you're a squeaky floor panel she stepped on. That's what I mean by "creepy."

I can't tell if Dar has even heard the rumors, or if she understands them. Sometimes I'm not even sure she's fluent in Earth Standard, but I'm also really not sure that she isn't. She does this thing where she'll look through you while you talk, like you're not even there or you're not sapient. But then sometimes you'll talk through a whole problem with someone else on the team and she'll speak up from across the room like she understood you all along.

I can't let her weirdness distract me, though. Mom told me not to underestimate Dar.

Next stop: Viokaron. It's what the Niralans call it. What Mom calls it. It's supposed to be a forgotten Niralan colony, or maybe a lost one. And it's also supposed to be supplying all those even-creepier non-speaking Niralans that Aqharan Bereth is supposedly making a fortune off of in the slave trade.

I don't know what it's supposed to be. But I know what it's going to be.

Viokaron is going to be the last place Dar Nantais ever sees.

Prologue

Piya Nahara knew almost nothing. But she knew, when she awoke that early summer morning, that her life was about to change.

She'd known it the last time her life had been about to change, too, only a few years ago. She'd woken with the same tension widening her eyes, the same pressure in her lungs that made air feel heavier, somehow. Not sharp; this was a dull ache, a wait-and-see ache rather than a go-find-out ache. *Nieai niees, la'darai dares.* Piya smiled. The repeating metaphors were her favorites.

Piya liked words. Piya liked mischief. And Piya loved knowing what would to happen before anyone else did. It almost made her feel grown up, which she almost was.

Last time, the change came from over her head, from the colony. Now she spent her days in the colony, with nothing over her head but the sky. So Piya went up.

She waited until she heard the door close, until the

doriie left for the central building, for her work with the Viidiari. Piya's mother would be in the kitchens by now, if Piya still had a mother, which she did not. Viokaron saw to that. Piya used to follow her mother about the compound, to set tables and fetch and carry, but the work no longer interested her even if the doriie allowed it, which she did not.

Piya's mother never said a word when Piya appeared in the kitchens. Not that Piya would have cared if her mother *did* say something, apart from the novelty of hearing her mother say *anything*. "Ela": it meant "silence," and Ela Nahara knew her name.

So did Piya.

Piya pried open the window sash, pushing it until the security notches in the sides stopped it moving, about twenty centimeters above the sill. She sucked in her breath and wriggled through, surprised at how much tighter the opening seemed. Getting onto the roof had been easier last week.

The sun shone gently that morning. A light breeze blew over the compound, bringing with it the smell of sublimating snow and just enough humidity to festoon the gutters with icicles. Piya patted down a mound of snow on the flat top of the roof and made herself a nest. The colony had only one sun. Koja – Piya's favorite person, after her mother – told her once that their homeworld had two suns. Piya could not imagine a world with twice the sun where the snow stayed put. But she believed it nonetheless.

The only change Piya needed now was her amaron.

Ola Nahara claimed Piya would never see any such thing; Viokaron saw to that as well, impersonal in its mercy and its justice, less a being than a thing, more a thing than the children who lay entombed beneath her feet. But nothing new could happen without it. Nothing new would happen until amaron did.

But change came from above. Why would that change come from above?

Piya's amaron mattered to her. It mattered to every child, every Niralan, since the emergence of *Lili Amarones*. It wasn't that Piya cared about tradition. She cared very little about the mysterious past, the not-now in which all the adults in her life found their being but about which they never spoke. But once she became an amaie, she would have a voice. The others would have to take her seriously. Or pretend to, anyway.

Piya possessed an unusually strong sense of self. Maybe it came from her name, which meant not "individual" or "singular" or "unique" – only *things* were talked about in that splintering manner – but "trickster," "enigma," "riddle."

Unlike the others, Piya was not treated as if she were a particular sort of person. Not a dutiful one like Ola, or easy to order around like Koja. Rather, adults treated Piya as if she were a particular sort of *non*-person, a cipher, a ghost. Piya grew up as a being without boundaries, and so she felt herself to be *all* boundaries, made up only of that which nobody else understood and which was therefore obscured to anyone but itself. *Piai pi'es*: to be impossible to catch.

Even Piya's connection to her mother meant almost nothing. Koja, who was a doctor, said it had to do with Ela's own silent peculiarities. But of her mother, Piya thought little and felt less. There wasn't much *to* think of anyone who was stuck with a name like "Ela." *Elaai elaes*: to sit silently. Piya herself heard those words so often, issued as a command – *Elaya elaes!* – that she had learned to hate them. Merely hearing her own mother's name made her feel trapped.

Piya Nahara was not sitting silently. Piya Nahara was *thinking*.

She was still thinking when the ship appeared.

Chapter 1

"Have you read the book yet?"

Dar Nantais did not look up from her breakfast. The question wasn't directed at her – though, without Dar, her crewmates wouldn't have asked it at all.

Per Interstellar Science custom, Dar had added her collection of books to the ship's common library when she'd joined the crew. Most of the books in her collection were technical manuals, which interested almost no one. Two of them were novels written by a friend of her grandmother's, which the ship's xenoanthropologist pounced on at once.

One of them was *the book*.

Print books stood out on a ship the size of the *Jemison*. Less than a dozen circulated among the crew, prized precisely for their analogue nature. *The book*, with its garishly-colored cover, stood out among the print books.

The cover attracted the commander's attention. He'd been the first to borrow it, fishing it out of Dar's bag before she'd unpacked properly.

"Haven't read a print book since college," he said, ducking his head like a child caught stealing candy.

The commander read it in a night, then reread it the next morning. He'd started reading it a third time when Rain de la Cruz, the ship's xenoanthropologist, caught a glimpse of the title.

Preferring a version whose print didn't skip and wriggle all over the page, de la Cruz looked up the book in the ship's database, only to discover that, according to the *Jemison*, the book did not exist. Neither did its author.

Undeterred, de la Cruz put in an information request to Archive. As a corporate state, Interstellar Science could access the Phobos Stack – the sum total of human knowledge, stored in the hollows of Mars's inner moon. De la Cruz sent the request casually, certain that Archive would send her a digital copy of the book in a week or two.

Instead, Archive sent her a terse note. The book did not exist. Neither did its author.

The book had been on board ten days when de la Cruz broke the news that no record of it or its author appeared in the Phobos Stack. Before her announcement, only de la Cruz and the commander had read it; suddenly, everyone on the crew scrambled to read it at once.

Despite being the book's owner, Dar Nantais hadn't read it. The book appeared in her mailbox on Station 32 one morning, and she'd transferred it to her small pile of personal objects without giving it a second thought. Koa sent her reading material at least once a month.

Nevertheless, Dar thanked *the book* for its existence. She had expected to spend her first month aboard the *Jemison* fending off rumors – about her position on the ship, her relationship with the commander, her species. Most humans never met a Niralan, much less served alongside one.

Once they realized Dar hadn't read the book and could only say that a cousin sent it to her, the *Jemison*'s crew left her alone. But the mystery of *the book* itself was too good to let go.

"I started it last night," said the ship's neurobiologist, Tenley Allman, to whom the question had been directed. "I'm only to the Pollock poem so far."

"You're killing me, Ten," said Jeri Edwards-Gan, the ship's official mission assistant and unofficial photographer. "Read faster."

"Normally I do," said Tenley. "But I started a list of all the things that looked like cultural references. I think you have to know them to really understand the book. But I can't find half of them in the padbase."

"Of course you didn't. Check out the first page. The book was written just a few decades before the Collapse. A lot of that stuff is probably gone forever."

"I found Anthony Burgess, Kurt Cobain, and *Finnegan's Wake*. I still have no idea who or what Jay Gatsby is."

Dar heard the scrape of a chair as de la Cruz joined Tenley and Jeri. "Chasing the references isn't going to help us figure out who the author is," de la Cruz said.

"I don't think I care yet," Tenley replied. "Besides,

I'm pretty sure there's more than just one author."

"No way."

"I'm serious." Another chair scraped the floor, and pages ruffled. "Here, look at this...."

Dar let the voices behind her subside into the general chatter. She returned her attention to the omnipad in front of her and the mysteries of the day ahead.

The *Jemison* had entered orbit around a small planet about six hours before the breakfast rush. The intelligence report Dar received from her mother, Jiya Nantais, called it *Viokaron*: Refuge. Asylum.

Early reports from Scan, which Dar skimmed until talk of *the book* interrupted her thoughts, showed a planet remarkably like Nirala. Oxygen-poor but sunlight-rich, Viokaron's surface was mostly frozen, save for a small temperate band near the equator. Scan also showed the makings of a colony, along with several hundred life signs.

One of the machine-learning nodes predicted, based on the life forms' movements relative to the planet's artificial structures, that they were likely sentient. Jiya's intelligence report predicted, with somewhat less confidence, that the planet's inhabitants were not only sentient but Niralan.

In a manner of speaking.

Ordinarily, Dar would have rejected Jiya's hypothesis outright. Niralans were scarce: The hamaya itself numbered only two hundred forty-seven. Granted, that number excluded both children and childless adults, neither of whom the senarie recognized as citizens. If even half the biosigns Scan detected were elders, then Viokaron alone boosted the hamaya's numbers by more than a third.

Ordinarily. But Dar's life had not been *ordinary* for over a month.

Dar last saw her mother on the Terminus, a high-security prison slash merchant outpost in Riyali space. By "merchants," the outpost meant slaves.

She'd seen them herself: Niralan children lined up for sale. Dozens of them. More children than she'd expect Nirala to produce in any one generation. The memory still made her dizzy.

Between them, Dar and Jiya could guess at only three possible sources. The first was Nirala herself. The second was New Barrow, the Niralan colony Jiya's mother had founded on Mars. The third was Viokaron.

Viokaron remained a question mark. So did Dar's orders from her mother. Make contact with Viokaron, determine whether the colony was the source of the Niralan slave trade, and…what? What did Jiya expect her to do with as many as a hundred of Nirala's children, stranded on a far-flung world?

A chair scraped across the metal flooring. Dar looked up as Richard Hayek, the ship's first officer and the other un-ordinary part of the previous month, joined her.

"Someone explain to me," Hayek said, "how that kid managed to hook a bioprinter to our cencom in a way that makes steak taste like steak, yet somehow we're still rationing coffee." He shook a fork out of its neatly-rolled napkin.

Dar slid her nearly-full coffee cup across the table to him.

He sighed but took the cup. "You don't have to do that."

"Cordry says we do," she replied. "Last time you showed up in engineering without your coffee, you made Lin cry."

"Lin was half-dressed and half drunk. Kid was lucky all I did was make him cry." Yet he smiled behind the cup.

Dar's mouth twitched in response, the closest she'd ever gotten to echoing the most ubiquitous of human gestures. The commander smiled more broadly, his eyes soft; he was, at present, the only person on board who could read her facial expressions, and it pleased him to have made her smile. She knew it would.

Despite having spent every day of the past month at his side and every night in his bed, Dar Nantais had not shed the habit of thinking of Richard Hayek as "the commander." She doubted she ever would.

The crew would have been scandalized to hear it. If they weren't so obsessed with *the book*.

The commander knew. It bothered him, but as with everything else that did, he said nothing. Their very first night together he asked her to call him by his first name, and the cavernous fluttering behind his breastbone told her *Call me Richard* was a request he'd never made of anyone and couldn't bear to hear rejected. He'd been embarrassed by his own dismay, ashamed to share it with her, so he pretended it didn't exist.

She didn't blame him for that. The human anteri-

or cingulate processed emotional pain the same way it processed physical pain. Putting a name to his feelings – like *fear* or *shame* or *vulnerability* or *loss* – would have had the same effect on his nervous system as punching himself in the teeth.

Dar would not have predicted that a species could both require social interaction to survive and obtain it solely through symbol-based communication – but somehow, humans did. Messily. Semi-consciously. She wondered how they could stand themselves.

"I see they're still talking about that book," the commander said.

"They like the mystery," Dar replied. *Like* was one of the Earth Standard words she classified in her head as "impossible" – words with no cognates in her own language or any substantive definition, yet that performed essential communicative functions. She kept a mental list of about two dozen, often framed as questions: *Do you like me? How are you doing? Are you all right?*

The commander shook his head. "Keeps them entertained, I guess. Never been good at literature myself."

Dar could relate.

The commander caught her eye briefly over the edge of the coffee cup. "You still haven't read it, have you?"

"Koa's always sending books we don't have time to read."

He shook his head, slowly. "I think you'd like it. Well – not like it, exactly. But I think you'd see a lot in it that the rest of us don't."

"How do you mean?" Dar asked, as conversational filler. Her curiosity about *the book* remained near zero.

The commander thought about this for a while, then shook his head. "You do language differently, that's all."

What that had to do with interpreting a human text, Dar didn't know and didn't ask.

"At least they're not talking about us," she said.

He snorted. "Should they be?"

It was Dar's turn to think rather than answer. *Yes* tipped her tongue, yet she couldn't say it. She knew the commander would ask her why *yes*.

She knew she should know why yes. She knew at one time she had known, had lived through the early days of partnering with a human that left every human acquaintance asking why. *How does that work? What do they talk about? Do they even like each other?*

Did she like the commander? She understood him. She needed him, the way she needed, on first waking, to know that her limbs were still attached and that her lungs could still breathe air. She could no more imagine leaving him than she could imagine misplacing her own body. Was that what they meant?

"Dar? *Dar. Commander.*" His voice cut through her reverie.

She started slightly and looked up. "Yes?"

The commander furrowed his eyebrows, like he always did when he was about to ask her an impossible question. She predicted which one it would be before he even asked it. "Are you all right?"

"I was thinking," she replied.

The furrow disappeared. "So you're fine," he said.

She felt the corner of her mouth twitch before she knew whether or not the commander's words were actually meant as a joke. His answering grin confirmed that they were.

"Do I like you?" she asked.

He paused midway through emptying her coffee cup. "What do you mean?"

It wasn't a lie if it would have happened but for *the book*, she reasoned. "The crew. They ask. The question is...complicated."

"It's a feeling," he said. "There isn't a cognate."

Of course. If growing up alongside humans hadn't taught her better, she would have presumed the species felt no emotions at all, just a series of elaborate movement rituals intended to mimic emotions' social effects. "So they're expecting behavior."

He smiled at this, though she failed to perceive the joke. "You could say that, yes."

"Of what kind?"

The smile faded. He raised an eyebrow, shifted in his chair. She'd baffled him.

She watched him think about her question, his eyes focused on the space just past her right shoulder, his eyebrows furrowed slightly.

"Now, for instance," he said. "They'd be expecting you to be leaning toward me, slightly. Smiling. Playing with your hair, maybe."

"My hair," she said.

He waved a hand, a gesture she'd learned to categorize mentally as *it's complicated*. "Making eye contact-" He broke off. "You know what, fuck it."

She blinked. The commander wasn't afraid to swear, but he tended to reserve profanities for situations that were actually profane. Was this one profane?

"You're fine," he said. "Just the way you are." The lines of his forehead softened. "I know how you feel about me. I'm the only one who matters."

She wasn't sure she agreed, but she recognized an attempt to be gentle when she saw it, and she appreciated it. She knew what it cost him to offer it.

The commander watched her for a moment. "Are you all right?"

Hadn't he just said she was fine? "What do you mean?"

He shook his head as if she'd caught him in a private moment. "I thought you'd be more nervous, is all." *About the planet*, he meant.

"To what purpose?"

The commander shook his head and mashed a bit of reconstituted scrambled egg with his fork. "Damn, I wish I had your sang-froid."

Sang-froid was not an Earth Standard word Dar knew, so she said nothing.

The commander swallowed. "You mind telling me what you plan to do down there?"

"What you do mean?" Dar asked again.

He pointed at her omnipad with his fork. "I mean we all know you're not just here as a good little corporate drone. What's Jiya asking you to do?"

Dar tapped her omnipad's screen blank, which made the commander smile for reasons she couldn't discern. "To confirm her suspicions. About this planet. Its inhabitants."

"The Terminus," the commander said. He shoved another forkful of eggs in his mouth. "Then what?"

"We have the same question," Dar said.

The commander nodded and began to speak again, but his voice disappeared under the squawk of the intercom. "Senior staff to the bridge."

"Go ahead," the commander said, pushing back his chair. He balanced her tray on top of his own, then drained the coffee cup. "I'm right behind you."

Chapter 2

The Viidan strode ahead of the other two, who nearly disappeared into the snowscape, their skin the same blue-tinged white that blanketed the ground. Niralans. Both were older than Dar, she saw as they drew closer: One had a full head of hair as white as her skin, while the other's blue-black hair had begun to develop streaks of white near the temples.

Their fingers laced through one another's. But as Dar stepped toward them, they shrank back in one motion, as if in fear of a flame.

Dar checked herself. She felt the weight of the commander's concern on her shoulder, heavy beneath the warmth of his palm.

"Oldie iaai?" the older Niralan asked: *Who are you?* Her choice of words – *ia*, you, one who is not of us – hurt worse than her recoil.

"Dar." She dind't bother to give them what Interstellar Science called her surname; she wore it on her face. Every Nantais possessed the same pattern of fine black lines that traced Dar's forehead and cheek, including the younger of the pair standing before her now. The elder's face bore only three lines, in a different pattern, framing knifelike blue eyes: Nahara.

"Dar," the older Niralan repeated. "What a difficult name."

Without contact, Dar couldn't tell whether her elder meant this in sympathy or sarcasm. She decided to ignore it.

"We're researchers with Interstellar Science," Dar continued, not bothering to translate. The captain and the commander spoke Niralanes well enough to follow the conversation. If the Viidan didn't, that was his problem. "This is our captain, Resa Molloy, and our first officer, Richard Hayek."

She felt a pang on saying Molloy's name and remembered too late that she should have let the captain answer the question, per first contact protocol.

"Where are they from?" the younger Niralan asked.

"What are you doing here?" the Viidan asked, also in Niralanes.

"Our home planet is called Earth," the captain said. "Our sensors indicated some areas of scientific interest on this planet. We're explorers. And you are—?"

"Tolva," the Viidan said, indicating himself, as if anyone else would have had such a name. He indicated the older and the younger Niralan in turn: "Ola. Koja."

Anpa hodevrine, Ola Nahara had said when Dar identified herself. A *difficult name*. Dar hadn't missed the commander's reaction, a jolt of surprise followed by acute unease: *hodevrine* meant difficult but also *dangerous*.

She could say the same for *Ola* and *Koja*: to *omit* and to *forget*. Difficult names – though, unlike Dar's, more likely to make trouble for others than for themselves.

"What sort of research do you do?" Tolva asked the captain. He spoke Niralanes better than the captain did; Dar might have mistaken him for a native speaker, save for the baritone pitch of his voice and a slight accent that reminded her of Tishkani. Was Tolva Tishkani, then? He didn't look it.

Molloy looked at Dar.

"Scientific," Dar said: the captain's vocabulary did not extend to specialized subject areas. "Mostly planetary: Geology, botany, and the like. We needn't interrupt-"

"You're welcome to interrupt," Tolva said. "In fact, any assistance you will provide us is welcome. Our power core in particular is trouble – we've had to deactivate it twice in the past month, and winter is coming. We don't see many visitors here, and those that do come are typically traders. Not much in the way of engineering skills." He sported a Tishkani's gregariousness too, the way they'd chat you up before they ripped out your throat or razed your entire neighborhood for spare minerals. Niralans kept long memories.

"What do you trade?" the captain asked.

"Raw materials, mostly. We've worked out a way to manufacture helium, of all things – but you'll see all that," Tolva said. "Let us show you the compound."

Molloy nodded. The commander caught Dar's eye and

raised an eyebrow, then fell into step behind the captain.

Dar followed them as far as the front door of the compound's largest building, three stories high and constructed primarily of glass and a dull grey-brown metal she couldn't immediately identify.

As she crossed the threshold, a flash of movement caught her attention. A third Niralan stood half-concealed behind a pillar just inside the doorway. Another Nahara, a child.

Dar pinched Ola's sleeve just hard enough to make the older Niralan pause. Ola and Koja turned as one, looking first at Dar and then at the girl as Dar indicated her presence.

"Piya," Ola said. The girl continued to watch them.

"Your daughter?" Dar asked. Ola affirmed.

Dar's first instinct was to reach for the girl's hands. Again she checked herself. She could only guess why Ola and Koja refused contact with her, but she knew that if they refused contact themselves, they would intervene if she tried to make contact with a child.

"Do you have children?" Ola asked her. It was one of the things she could have learned simply by taking Dar's hand. For that reason, the question grated: Dar had not spent a lifetime among humans simply to replicate their symbol-based imitation of sociability with her own people.

"No," Dar replied, the flat click of the tongue that signaled negation in Niralanes.

Ola motioned toward a pair of long, low benches set to the right of the building's entrance, between two pillars near the center of the entrance space. They were upholstered in fabric as gray as the floor and walls that surrounded them. The view from the adjacent window consisted mostly of compound wall, and so provided scant relief.

Dar sat. Ola and Koja sat facing her. Piya Nahara stayed on her feet, hovering at the edge of Dar's peripheral vision like a hallucination or a ghost.

For a moment, Ola and Koja appeared to ignore Dar, their heads inclined toward one another, though neither spoke. Dar recognized the pose: They were working something out between themselves.

Ola broke the silence. "We have a request of you," she said.

"Our numbers have been dwindling here for decades. At present there are only three of us left. And only an amara can make another amara."

Dar didn't need contact to understand. Ola had just asked her to facilitate Piya's amaron.

Amaron: The transition from a nonspeaking childhood to a speaking adulthood. The process was at once neurological and mythic, bringing a child into the world of adult movement, action, and self-determination by triggering rapid neuron growth in key areas of the Niralan brain, including the speech centers. It changed the child to an adult; it gave the adult a lifelong responsibility.

That Ola and Koja would ask Dar Nantais, a stranger they refused even to touch, to perform Piya's amaron told her everything.

"What about your daughter?" Dar asked Koja. Koja Nantais had said nothing about her own family so far, but Dar could reason from premises: If Koja were still an amaie, she'd have done Piya's amaron herself.

"Dead," Koja said, her voice lost between the metal pillars. "None of us survive long here." *Vela*: it meant *survive*, but to survive by hiding, to stay in a safe place.

"There are no others," Ola said. "We've watched the visitors for years. We hoped, but hope starved until now."

Ininai inines. Or, as the commander might have put it, *beggars can't be choosers*.

"We need to consider," Dar said.

"Please," Ola pressed. The word surprised Dar: *yaeya* was not a word Niralan elders said to amaie. "We will be lost here without you."

Dar felt the floor shift beneath her feet, although no outside force shook the room. She stood.

"We need to find our captain," she said, and took advantage of Ola's refusal to touch her to leave without being stopped.

She found the others by following Tolva's voice, which took on an odd booming quality once the trio left the entryway. Following the sound, she saw why: The corridor ahead of her bore no resemblance to the rest of the building. It was built of an entirely different metal, blue-gray in color and close. It gave her an almost museumlike chill.

"The power cores were rebuilt over time from the remains of the ship's engine," Tolva said as Dar rejoined the commander, trailing slightly behind the captain and the Viidan. "Our ancestors built around the intact parts of the engine complex rather than disturb the cores."

"You crashed here?" Dar asked. The commander placed a hand on her shoulder again, saving himself from having to voice his thoughts. He'd known where she was, but he'd worried about her nonetheless.

"Our ancestors did," Tolva said. "We've been here 96 rotations."

Dar recalled the planet's period data, buried in the reports from Scan, and did a quick mental calculation. Viokaron's first settlers had arrived just over three hundred Earth Standard years prior.

She looked up, intending to ask Tolva where the crashed ship had come from, but the Viidan moved on to another topic. "We've taken these combustion coils offline so we can reach the heating elements. As you can see, the problem is less one of mechanics than control." He disappeared inside the coil chamber. His voice disappeared with him.

The captain stuck her head inside the coil chamber as Tolva continued to narrate. Dar, meanwhile, examined a readout on the side of the chamber's exterior wall.

"There's a problem with the control software," she said, raising her voice slightly to be heard inside the coil chamber.

"Precisely," Tolva said. "What we need is someone who understands both ends of the problem – and who doesn't mind years of repairs by people who didn't understand either end."

The captain stepped out of the chamber and joined Dar at the readout screen. "Can you fix it?" she asked.

The question didn't process at first; Dar caught its meaning and shook her head just as the captain started to repeat herself. "Not alone. But I think Erin Lang can do the job."

Molloy's snort told Dar what the captain thought of their newest passenger. "If you think so."

"She has the coding skills. And she's no stranger to jury-rigged power systems." *Especially not when they run on Eikore'es code*, she omitted.

Molloy stepped out of Tolva's way as the latter emerged from the remains of the three hundred year old engine. "We may have someone who can help you."

"By all means," Tolva said. "Now, if you'll come with me, I will introduce you to...." His enunciation faded into the echo as he entered the hallway, not bothering to check whether anyone was following him.

The captain caught Dar's attention as they followed the Viidan. "Head back to the ship and start organizing teams with Benby. We'll be back shortly. Chirp if you need anything."

"You won't need assistance?" Dar asked.

The captain nodded toward the commander. "We'll survive."

The commander squeezed Dar's shoulder one last time as she passed him. His face told her he'd overheard the captain's command; his touch told her he was full of questions – and that his earlier unease had, if anything, grown.

Dar could do little about either one in the moment. She squeezed back and turned right out of the metal hallway as the commander and the captain turned left, following Tolva.

Ola and Koja sat on the same entryway bench. This time, Dar didn't give her elders a chance to recoil.

Her fingers darted out, taking Ola's free hand in her right and Koja's in her left. It took all three only a moment to recognize one another.

Not family. Not Niralans. La'Isshai.

"La'ilaai Nirala," Ola whispered. *They, not we, are Nirala.*

"Nirala von," Dar replied. *For her survival.*

Chapter 3

To: Koa Nantais, Ambassador
From: Dar Nantais, ISS *Jemison*

Re: Reservations

Have I any business with amaron?

Her name is Piya Nahara. She knows almost nothing. We grew up isolated from the hamaya; Piya Nahara has grown up alone.

All of which ought to be relevant to my question, and none of which is. I need to know if I'm making the right choice — and I repeat I for emphasis, as I cannot help but feel I will set myself against the hamaya by siding with this child.

> And yet. Only an amaie can make another amaie, and I am the only amaie in sight.
>
> I question amara itself. Amaron is cruel; we warn our children of every pitfall of a speaking adulthood except the one that will actually trap them. We tell them everything but we tell it in code, as if Lili Amarones could ever do anything but reproduce the conditions of our own hereditary oppression. By the time they — we — understand the trap, we've already begun laying it for the next generation.
>
> There has to be another way. Please advise.
>
> **Nirala sodeva.**
>
> **Dar**

Dar set her omnipad aside and lifted her comb from its place on the commander's headboard.

She'd spent every night of the past three weeks in his bed, or he in hers. Normally it relieved her to retire with him for the night, to stop processing his words through the extensive mental database of human perceptions she'd built up over her lifetime. Sometimes she preferred him when he yelled; the more gently he tried to say things, the more she struggled to understand him.

Tonight, however, she faced a more difficult problem.

Dar knew *Lili Amarones*, of course. Every adult Niralan did. *Lili Amarones* was the foundational myth of her people, the story and instructions of existence. Instructions, Dar discovered after the fact, that did almost nothing to actually prepare one for a speaking adulthood.

Once, not long after her own amaron, Dar had called *Lili Amarones* "programming instructions for Niralans." "They teach amaie to function in a society where the ability to speak does not imply an equivalent right to be heard," she said. Jiya, unamused, refused to acknowledge her daughter for a week.

When Ola asked whether she would take on Piya's amaron, Dar's first thoughts had been for the hamaya. Ordinarily, amaie were matched carefully with their amiie, the children they guided. Eri Nereved had been Dar's amaie precisely because Dar needed Eri's stability as a counterweight to her own curious contrariness. Dar Nantais serving as amara to Piya Nahara – it was a volatile combination. Jiya would have vetoed it at once: *not in the best interests of Nirala*.

Now, sitting in bed in the commander's quarters, her hair cascading like a child's around her shoulders and her clothes folded atop the dresser, Dar began to wonder whether Piya Nahara's amaron was in the best interests of Dar Nantais.

Amaron forged a lifelong bond between the two participants, a sense of responsibility that superseded responsibilities to bonded partners and deferred only to responsibilities to other members of one's own kiiste.

To guide Piya through amaron would bind her to Dar forever – and vice versa.

She heard the squeak of the tap. The crash of water into the shower slowed to a trickle, then silence.

She didn't want the responsibility of Piya Nahara. But to refuse it would be to allow the memory of Viokaron to die completely.

Perhaps that's not a bad thing.

The commander leaned out of the open bathroom door, toothbrush in hand. He studied her for a moment, then frowned.

"What's on your mind?" he asked, and stuck the toothbrush in his mouth.

"Motherhood," Dar replied. Hayek choked.

She heard the water turn on, followed by a clatter as he spat a mouthful of toothpaste, toothbrush and all, into the sink. He coughed a few times, then reappeared in the doorway.

"What?" he asked.

"Amaron."

The commander frowned again. "Read me in on that."

Dar gathered her thoughts. Translation never came easily to her; humans in particular seemed to assume that their understanding of her words equated somehow to the real thing, rather than standing at several removes from the original.

"It's what you call....coming of age. Only it's not merely symbolic. The ritual itself triggers the growth of neurological connections in the speech centers and in other areas of the brain."

"It's the thing that makes your children capable of speaking," said the commander. "Which is the thing that makes them not children."

"Yes."

He looked relieved. She must have misinterpreted his face.

"Why are you thinking about this?" he asked.

"Piya Nahara," Dar replied. "Ola Nahara's daughter. She's at the right age, but there's no one else who can stand as her amara."

"Koja?" the commander asked.

"She's had a child. Only an amara can make another amara."

The commander reached for the tap, turning it off without leaving the doorway. "And you're thinking about motherhood as a way to get out of it, or...?"

"Not exactly. Amaron – it's not an episode. It's a commitment. Piya Nahara would become my responsibility."

"She'd be an adult, though," the commander said. "Right?"

"Yes. But my responsibility, nonetheless." Dar pulled the blanket closer around her shoulders. "Ordinarily, the choice of amara is a considered one. This is chance. It's a bad combination."

"You're sure? How much time did you spend with this girl?" The commander emerged from the bathroom, drying his hands on a towel.

"Her name is Piya Nahara."

The look the commander gave her told Dar he didn't understand, but he also didn't want to risk a confrontation by pushing back.

"What do you plan to do?" he asked, hanging the towel over the back of a chair.

"I don't know yet," Dar said as Hayek settled himself on the edge of the bed, beside her. "If I leave her voiceless, this colony and its memories will die. If I consent..."

The commander took her hands in his, saving her from having to finish her thought.

"Let me ask you a different question," he said after a moment. "That readout on the coil chamber. Eikore'es?"

"Yes." The commander had encountered the language before, but only briefly. It surprised Dar that he learned to identify it so quickly.

"What's that doing out here? More chance?"

As far as Dar was concerned, the commander already knew too much about this aspect of her people's history. "We lost a ship, once," she edited. "Or rather, the Tishkani did, during the collapse of the Second Empire."

"Eikore'es," the commander said. "In the manner of the empire."

"Yes."

"There were Niralans on board?"

"Ten." She intended not to tell him, but the raw energy flowing from his hands to hers told her that if she omitted the truth, he'd only assume worse. "They were La'Isshai."

She recognized the commander's reaction before the Earth Standard words registered: aversion, mixed with *fear*. "That's why they avoided touching you."

"Yes. They didn't know I'm one of them. They feared they might contaminate me."

"After three hundred years?"

"It can't be bred out of us," Dar reminded him. His aversion turned to something like sorrow.

Niralans were not, by their nature, violent. An instinct for self-preservation had been bred into a handful of them during the Second Empire, controlled with rigorous training in the deadly arts and in the mental discipline required to kill only where, when, how, and whom the senarie demanded.

But that instinct for self-preservation threatened the identity of a people whose biological need for communion drove them to seek consensus even to the point of immolation. To preserve the hamaya, the La'Isshai were forbidden to return home, and prohibited from so much as holding hands with anyone who didn't share their defective ancestry.

"Do you think that ship has anything to do with the Terminus?" the commander asked. It was a fair question: the Terminus's computer systems also ran Eikore'es code.

"Too soon to tell," Dar said, "but if they're who I think they are, no. They've probably been here for centuries. Though that needn't have stopped them from trading with anyone willing to make the trip."

"Do you think Ola and Koja-" the commander began,

then stopped himself. The pang that passed from his hand to hers told her why. *Do you think they're selling their own children into slavery*, he meant.

"No," Dar said. "Though if I have to reevaluate, I will. They have the means and opportunity; motive remains a cipher."

"They might be lying to you," the commander said.

Ola Nahara almost certainly was, a factor Dar had already considered. Yet Ola's hands communicated an honest urgency. Ola may not be telling Dar the entire story, but she told enough of it for Dar to believe the parts she'd heard.

She started as his frustration slid beneath her fingernails like sandpaper.

"What is it?" she asked.

His smile missed his eyes. "I just wish you'd read the book, is all."

"What does the book have to do with-"

"Nothing," he said, so quickly Dar was certain Hayek was lying to her. "Forget I asked. Just...don't do anything reckless, all right?"

But Dar felt something like anger at the back of her skull, a sensation that flowed up her arm from his, laced with an acid panic. She was tired. Tired from her day; tired of trying to guess at him.

"What are you afraid of?" she asked.

His reaction hit her in the face like a fistful of gravel, though his hands didn't move. "Dar, you know what I'm afraid of."

"I'm not going anywhere."

"I need you to be safe."

Ludicrous. They were thousands of light-years from their respective home worlds, required by the terms of their contracts and their very survival to make contact with any number of hostile sentient species. They'd run afoul of several dangerously vindictive parties, injected themselves into a lost civilization with no use for them, and relied for all of it on an outdated processor and a few layers of foil to separate them from the unforgiving vacuum of space.

Words formed behind her jaw: *You're confusing the safe with the familiar*. But she didn't say them. She predicted he would categorize them, as humans often did, as *arguing for the sake of it*.

"Ola may lie to me by omission," Dar said, "but she won't harm me. She needs me as much as we need her."

"You know that now. You didn't this morning." But the gravel-whipped sting was giving way to something closer to his default emotional state: A silent fog, a grey swamp. Despair.

She watched him.

A moment later he looked at her again. "It's just – I thought this had started to make sense, but now that we're here...." He shook his head. "Maybe you'll never make sense to me. I don't know."

"My grandmother married a human. He said the same thing." So had someone else, someone she knew once but could no longer place. A mass of auburn curls flitted through her memory; it sank beneath the depths as she reached for it.

"Come to bed," she said after a moment. She knew it softened him to be asked.

He sighed, but stripped off his shirt.

She preferred him like this, she thought as he folded his body around hers beneath the sheets. She preferred them both this way: quiet, connected, neither one of them struggling to put their interior worlds into the gravel-rough foreign structure of words. She had met humans to whom verbalization came easily, whose interior worlds seemed made of words, their own memories or self-awareness inaccessible without them. But not his. Whenever he spoke, it was with a rising serrated edge of effort within the bone that told her speech was not his native tongue either.

In bed together, there was no need to talk. They understood one another.

Piya Nahara knew almost nothing about the visitors. But she intended to find out.

Ola's refusal to touch Dar had not surprised Piya, but Ola's request that Dar Nantais perform Piya's amaron did. Ordinarily, the adults did not conduct Piya's business in front of her; they made their decisions behind closed doors and informed Piya after the fact.

As a result, Piya Nahara knew how to sneak around behind the adults. The alcove behind the door was one of her favorite hiding places; if she concentrated on becoming a pillar, she could hide there for hours while

Tolva and the others went back and forth with traders, sharing stories and information Piya would ordinarily never be allowed to hear.

Piya ticked off on her fingers each item she had learned about the alien visitors today. They spoke Niralanes, albeit badly. They came from a planet that trapped autumn sunlight and winter moss beneath its people's skin. Some of them were built like Tolva, narrow in the hips and wide in the shoulders, trapped in perpetual adolescence without the ability to bear children of their own: The aliens, like Viidans, spent resources on superfluous members. She could call them people because at least one of them, the one whose hand rarely left Dar's shoulder, was people.

Piya Nahara learned all these things without the aliens ever once seeing her. But Dar Nantais saw her.

Piya paused when it came to classifying Dar Nantais. Dar's name wasn't enough. Dar's face, perversely, was even less helpful. She held it the way the aliens did, the muscles tense beneath the skin as if she needed them ready for some kind of use.

Worst, Dar hadn't flinched when none of them offered to touch her. Dar Nantais was as sick as they were. Ola Nahara had failed to contain the contagion.

Ola said you couldn't see faravajie, but Piya swore she could smell it on Dar.

Piya Nahara knew what was at stake. She'd overheard Tolva discussing terms with the captain of the last tradeship, just over two months ago. *Finish this shipment, and we'll pay you well for your trouble.* Piya hadn't missed the leer on the tradeship captain's face, nor had she misunderstood the accounts file Tolva carelessly left on his desk. By *pay you well* he meant *pay you in Piya*.

But Piya Nahara was no use to a tradeship captain if she could talk.

Piya Nahara didn't panic. Piya Nahara hatched plans of her own. Dar's cooperation would help, but if Dar didn't cooperate, it didn't matter. Piya never relied on the cooperation of adults.

The clock on the headboard glowed as the commander snored softly beside her. Dar watched the numbers flip past until the obvious solution presented itself.

If Viokaron was selling its children, it had exhausted its supply. Piya Nahara remained the only one in danger of enslavement, and that danger pressed only as long as she remained a child.

Piya Nahara, by name and nature, was little more than a ghost. She could remain unseen, and she possessed a Nahara's curiosity.

Dar couldn't rely on Ola or Koja to tell her the truth about Viokaron, even if they knew it. *Anpa hodevrine*.

But she could rely on Piya. As much as anyone could rely on a phantom.

The matter settled itself. Dar rolled over, her head pressed against the commander's shoulder, and slipped into sleep.

Chapter 4

Unregistered space was 99.99999999999999999999 9999999999999999999 percent empty, and the remainder existed solely to piss him off.

This, Hayek knew, was an absurdity. Not to mention egocentric, with a pettiness he despised. Space was mostly nothing, and even the parts that were something were not interested in him. It was only when he woke up feeling like *this* that he thought everything within arm's reach could use a good solid punching.

This could be described as frustration, if one was feeling generous; a clusterfuck, if one wasn't.

He wasn't.

Ordinarily, waking up beside her came as a relief. He kept count of the days it happened, the mornings in which she hadn't disappeared in favor of anyone who deserved her more than he did.

Forty-three. Including this one.

Being in Dar's presence put each part of Hayek's mind back where it ought to go. It helped him wake up each morning momentarily unencumbered by the task of ignoring the emotions he couldn't name and naming the emotions he couldn't ignore. Every day he fought to make sense of his inner world, and every day he failed. It was his greatest battle – one that, until Dar appeared in his life, Hayek fought entirely on his own.

Once when was five, his mother smacked him across the face for crying. "Men keep it shut," she'd said. It wasn't the worst lie she ever told him, but it was the most pernicious.

He'd known it was a lie when she said it, but he'd believed it. He believed it to this day. He hated himself for it.

Easy to believe on a morning like this, he thought as he stumbled to the bathroom. He felt like he usually did after a long day of translation: A rusting frame with a brain made of ration-pack sludge, angry at something but unable to name what.

Dar. The urge to blame her rose in his throat like bile. He forced it back down. Babysitting his emotions wasn't her job.

He glanced at her in his bed, and anger gave way to concern. Normally he woke up knowing her feelings better than he knew his own. It wasn't her responsibility to sort him out, but she did. Usually.

What happened?

He took a step back toward his bunk when he heard the sheets rustle. The bedsprings creaked as she sat up, and he returned to the sink. He'd talk to her in a moment.

Today would be a good day for some combat drills, he thought as he shaved. The crew were far more assiduous about their daily conditioning since the most recent incident, but it paid to keep them on their toes. It also gave him an excuse to yell, and he felt like yelling.

He turned the water off and reached for a towel.

She had already left when he emerged from the bathroom. The silence in the room felt like reproach.

God fucking dammit, he thought and reached for his boots.

Yelling was in vogue that morning: a raised voice, shrill with suppressed tears, met him the moment he stepped into the corridor.

"...not talking about this anymore," Erin Lang said. Her back was to Hayek; she was yelling at an open doorway a few yards down the corridor, which led to Senior Engineer Cordry's quarters. Her voice echoed off the dull brown walls. "Maybe we just shouldn't talk at all."

Hayek thought he heard a protest from somewhere within Cordry's quarters, but Lang didn't stick around to hear it; she stalked off, her long blonde hair swishing behind her as she rounded the corner. Hayek nearly smiled in spite of himself. He'd been that young once.

Not that I'm doing much better, he thought as his own quarters loomed over his shoulder. He slid the door closed and headed for the mess hall. At least Dar was still talking to him.

He caught up to her in the breakfast line, managing a surreptitious squeeze of her hand as they both reached for trays. Her eyes smiled in response; his heart leapt.

"Wondered where you went," he remarked.

"Cencom-3."

Something to do with the mess in the ship's central computer core, then. No surprise; the problem had kept her awake for several nights already. Hayek understood none of it. He'd even given up trying to parse the weekly reports Dar filed on her team's progress. As the *Jemison*'s computational linguist and its best programmer – and the reason the cencom was in this state – Dar was the natural choice.

The ship still ran. That was all Hayek needed to know.

They loaded scrambled eggs and bacon onto their trays. The eggs were reconstituted, as usual, but Cordry had leveraged some of Dar's cencom work to adapt the mess hall bioprinter for proteins that tasted like actual meat.

Dar skipped the toast. Hayek considered it, then took a slice. Even reprocessed calories were calories. Besides, after fourteen years in deep space, he barely recalled what real bread tasted like.

He sat down across from Dar at the smallest table, looking forward to a leisurely breakfast. His surly mood faded. For once, Hayek looked forward to his day.

"Commander, you are not going to *believe* what I found in aux-six last night."

Fuck it. These kids were doing combat drills till he was hoarse.

Oblivious to Hayek's mood, Cordry turned a chair around and flopped into it, passing Dar an omnipad almost before she'd set down her tray. "Look at that neuron profile."

Dar disappeared into the screen at once, as Hayek knew she would; Dar's special interests included machine learning, and Cordry had belonged to her team for a decade. More than that: Cordry, only 14 years old when assigned to Station 32, grew up under Dar's tutelage. The kid was a prodigy.

"...I was thinking, last night, if there's a way to route the biolab's standing functions through aux-six as well, given the current state of the S-drives, but then I realized that it'd be much easier to connect via the pin ports if we had the right interlocks, which I guess we could print but that'd set the schedule back a few weeks, and I know Jeri was waiting on parts...."

A shout from the kitchen did the impossible: It made Cordry shut up.

Dar and Hayek stood in the same movement.

Crewmembers dodged out of the way as the commanders hastened toward the source of the noise.

At first, Hayek didn't understand what he was seeing. It looked as if the whole kitchen was wriggling. Then he blinked and realized: the kitchen wasn't moving. It was merely covered, in a tangled mass of pale yellow strings – no, worms – or –

"Pasta," Dar said quietly behind him.

It was. The kitchen floor was a mass of limp spaghetti noodles, and more were spilling from a hatch in the wall to the right, which Hayek recognized as the output for the new bioprinter.

"It just went nuts," said Grace Lehou, the team's geneticist, who was on breakfast duty that morning. She pushed her braids over her shoulder. "Just started up out of nowhere."

"Was anyone back there?" Hayek asked.

Lehou gestured at Cohen, the astrophysicist, and at Lang, both wearing the disposable kitchen aprons that indicated they were on food duty. "We were all standing right here."

"Could be a problem with the interface," Dar said. Hayek looked at her. "We'll take a look after briefing."

"I don't get it," Cohen said. "It's not even programmed for starches yet."

Hayek nodded. "We're late," he said. "I'll send a few people to help you clean up."

"Appreciate it, commander," Lehou replied, looking glumly at the noodles spilling onto her feet.

Pasta. Of all the weird glitches. But then, maybe it'd be a net gain. Hayek had nearly forgotten what real noodles tasted like, too.

He settled back into his seat as Dar tapped the omnipad's screen, then passed it to Cordry. "Track those bands against the bioprinter's output. What do you see?"

"You mean the pasta thing?" Cordry asked, taking the omnipad back.

"Yes."

The engineer frowned at the screen. "You really think those are related?"

"That is the problem we're attempting to solve."

Cordry swiped the screen a few times, frown deepening. "Because I was messing with the Ling-Hernandez generator in aux-six earlier this morning – like, four a.m., I couldn't sleep – but I didn't think...*pasta*. Weird." The engineer looked up. "Do you know anything about classical animation?"

Dar shook her head, but Cordry wasn't waiting for an answer; the only thing the kid did better than engineering was switching topics rapidly and for no discernible reason. "Erin and I were watching – well. It's complicated."

Hayek caught Dar's eye, saw the amusement there.

"Anyway, last night," Cordry continued, "before it got complicated, we had a date night in my quarters. Heated up a couple ration packs, those mystery ones the labels fell off of. Turned out to be spaghetti bolognaise. Erin thought it was great, because her movie pick turned out to be this old-school piece about these two dogs that fall in love, and there's a scene where they have a spaghetti dinner."

"Dogs," Dar said.

"Classical animation," Cordry said. "I guess those used anthropomorphized animals a lot. Erin can explain it; she's mad for that sort of thing. Hand-drawn stills, absurd flicker rates, visible grain, all that. Apparently it's a real art form. A large part of the twentieth century was devoted to it."

"What happened to the dogs?" Dar asked.

"The dogs?"

"In the classical animation."

"To tell you the truth," Cordry said, "we didn't get that far."

Hayek choked back a laugh.

"Anyway, I was thinking about it the whole time I was on the Ling-Hernandez generator. Like, how symbolic it was, that our dinner and the dinner in the scene were the same. And-"

"Cordry," Dar interrupted. "Are you suggesting the cencom read your mind?"

Cordry hesitated. "When you put it that way, it sounds absurd."

"What I mean," Dar said, "is that aux-six and the bioprinter aren't really what's bothering you."

Cordry slumped. "Am I that obvious? I mean – the reason I was down in cencom-3 in the first place was because I couldn't sleep. Because of Erin.

"It's – we've – been kind of on-again off-again for a while now. Because we weren't always on the same projects. I mean, we weren't always on the same planet, even."

Funny way to describe piracy, Hayek thought.

"But then we both ended up here, and I thought we could make a thing of it, right? Like, I thought she'd actually care about – at least, I thought things were going really well. That spaghetti thing. I couldn't have *planned* that but you just know we'll be laughing about it for years. Or I thought we would, but then.... I was reading the book because I couldn't sleep, but then Erin woke up and got all pissed at me that I'm reading it without her, so I left, and apparently that made it *worse.*" The engineer paused.

"If it is a coincidence," Cordry continued, "it's weird, isn't it? First the mystery meals, then the movie, then the bioprinter. When do coincidences become a pattern?"

Dar inclined her head slightly, the way she did when she was waiting for someone to answer their own question.

"It's the kind of thing you'd find in that book," Cordry said, indicating the engineering toolbag that rested against the table leg. The garish cover of *the book* peeped from the top of the outer pocket.

"You haven't been reading to the cencom, have you?" Hayek asked, joking.

Cordry blinked. "No. Why would I do that?"

Hayek shook his head.

Meanwhile, Dar entered a few more keystrokes into Cordry's omnipad. She shoved it back in the engineer's direction.

Cordry stood at once, rattling the table. "That's it. Thanks, commander."

"Should I even ask what you did?" Hayek asked in the sudden void caused by Cordry's disappearance, tool bag and all.

"Great engineer," Dar said. "Terrible programmer."

They ate in peace for a few moments. Hayek remembered what he wanted to ask her. He leaned forward.

"Commander?"

For a moment he thought Cordry had returned. Then he registered the plastic kitchen apron and the waist-length blonde hair: The voice belonged to Erin Lang.

"I have a plan," Lang said. "For the – combustion coils? In the compound? I think we can fix the system and make it run more efficiently." She offered Dar a smudged omnipad.

Dar scanned the proffered screen without touching it. "Go ahead."

"Thanks!" Lang danced on the spot for a moment. "And can you...check on it? When I need help? It's just – you don't have to be there or anything, I just want to make sure I get it right."

Dar nodded once.

"Thanks – I mean, thank you, commander!" Lang hugged her omnipad and skittered away.

"I think you intimidate her," Hayek said.

"We'll be late for briefing," Dar replied.

So they would, he realized; around them, people were already stacking chairs and pushing tables together, converting the cargo-bay-turned-multipurpose room into its midmorning incarnation as a meeting space. He let Dar take his tray and stood, shoving their table against the others and lining the chairs up alongside.

Briefing was brief. Benby was taking a team to the surface to discuss the local flora with Koja Nantais and a team of Viidan scientists. Hayek had his plan to run combat drills approved before it occurred to him that perhaps he should accompany the research team. Benby's Tishkani was passable, but Hayek doubted that it extended to botanical minutiae.

Still, Benby seemed confident, and Hayek's mood improved somewhat when Dar volunteered to stay aboard and supervise Cordry's work on the bioprinter glitch. If Dar wasn't going to the surface, she wouldn't get in more trouble there, either.

He shook his head as the mass scraping of chairs against deck plating announced the meeting's end.

Hayek had miscalculated. By the time Molloy and Benby chose their teams, over half the crew had gone outside.

Hayek saw no point in running defensive drills with the handful who were currently awake. Instead, he tossed himself into a chair at Ops to stare at his ever-expanding pile of paperwork.

He'd barely finished working out which of his reports was the most overdue when the comm beeped at him.

He smacked the console button with the back of his omnipad. "Hayek."

"Change of plans," Molloy's voice said. "I need you out here after all."

He sat up. Both Benby and de la Cruz spoke Tish Kan, and Molloy's Niralanes was as good as his. "What's going on?"

"Their botanists only speak Pitonk'ol."

Hayek leaned toward the speaker. "Say that again."

"Their botanists. Only speak. Pitonk'ol."

He'd heard her correctly the first time, but he'd never heard of the language. He tapped the screen of his omnipad, rendering the syllables in the Viidan standard alphabet as he said, "How's that?"

"Politics. Some kind of schism. They obviously don't want to talk about it. I need a translator, Hayek. Stat."

The omnipad was not telling him anything he wanted to hear. "One problem."

There was a moment of dead silence, then Molloy's aggravation leaked through the comm circuits. "Don't tell me you don't speak it."

"Never heard of it."

"You're my godsdamned linguist, Hayek."

"Do you know how many languages exist on Viida?" he asked. "Four thousand, two hundred and twelve, at their last census. I speak fifteen of those. This one's not one of them, and it's not related to any of the ones I do know, either. According to the padbase, it's practically extinct."

"Well, it's doing fine here," Molloy said, "so you'd better figure something out. Now."

He stood. "I'm on my way."

He'd nearly made it to the door of the bridge before Molloy's voice crackled over the comm again. "Hayek."

He turned. "Yeah."

"Ask Nantais."

Hayek frowned. "I don't think even she knows this one."

"Ask her anyway," the captain replied. "She's full of surprises."

That's true.

"On it," he said, and headed for cencom-3.

Chapter 5

Amapa't la'dar, Koja said whenever a ship arrived. *There's no accounting for aliens.* She used it as an excuse: *amapa't la'dar,* as she sent Piya to fetch her tools or make some tea or clean some little-used storage room. Any errand, no matter how contrived, so long as it sent Piya in the opposite direction to the ships or the teams that worked with them.

When the new aliens showed up, Piya heard those words in her head again, as clearly as if Koja herself occupied Piya's mind. *Amapa't la'dar.*

There may be no accounting for alien behavior, but Piya brooked no excuse for Koja's continued interference with curiosity, either.

Piya kept places to hide herself and her things all over the compound. They proved useful for one who had to steal everything she knew. Only a few of them actually kept Piya from physical sight; most, like her hiding place just inside the compound's main doors, offered her the opportunity to go unnoticed rather than offering physical concealment.

Most people looked right through Piya when she hid in these places. Dar Nantais had looked right *at* her. The memory made her think twice about today's hiding place.

The core complex called her. The tangle of pipes and conduits that spread from the core chambers interfered with most lines of sight. Since the previous morning, the aliens had been visiting the malfunctioning core in a steady stream. If she tucked herself behind the pipes, Piya knew, she could watch the aliens without being detected herself.

The two aliens currently bouncing their voices off the metal walls weren't the two Piya saw with Dar Nantais the morning before. The mere sight of those two fascinated her: The shorter alien with skin like autumn loam; the taller one scarcely lighter, but tinged with a warmth that suggested spring sunlight lay beneath his skin.

Those two, the first two aliens of their kind Piya had ever encountered, looked different from the two working on the core now. These two looked oddly alike: same narrow build, same long thin limbs, same pink-orange skin and hair like limp grain. One wore shorter hair than the other. Both talked nonstop.

"Hey, can you pass me that wrench?"

"Why are these radiation levels so *high*? Is someone trying to tap into the core somewhere?"

Piya crept closer. The short-haired alien knelt beside an open access panel at the base of the main core. A few feet away, the long-haired alien stood beside the core's control circuits, holding some kind of flat-screened control device.

"I don't know, check the signal board," the short-haired alien said to the inside of the access panel.

"It's not showing anything, but for all we know, that's broken too," the long-haired alien said. "Anyway, don't go in there till we figure out how to flush the thing. These Eikore'es cores can be flushed, right?"

Piya let their language wash over her, reveling in its sound. Koja's campaign to keep her away from all alien visitors deprived Piya of their languages as well. It chafed at her. Yesterday's aliens spoke Tishkani and even some Niralanes. Their pronunciation butchered the latter, but it also proved that the aliens had their own language, one Piya had never heard. She longed to understand it.

These aliens made noises Piya had never heard, hard-soft-hard-soft, like snowmelt running over gravel. From its sounds, so like the errors in pronunciation made by yesterday's aliens, she guessed the short-haired and long-haired aliens spoke their own language.

She didn't understand a word of it. But that didn't stop her from creeping close enough to watch the aliens at work.

"C," the long-haired alien said. "Are you even listening to me?"

"What?" The short-haired alien's head had disappeared into the access panel.

"I *said*, what's the pressure rating on those lines? The blue ones on your left?"

A pause. "They're not marked. Should be about 1.4, though."

"Should be? About? What am I supposed to do with that?"

Both aliens' voices grew sharper, words slapping the air with more force. Piya let the back of her mind absorb them as the front halted, its attention riveted.

Piya Nahara saw a book.

A book saw Piya Nahara.

"You know it's going to be between 1.4 and 1.8. I thought you were just running a simulation anyway."

"Yeah, *a* simulation, C. I don't want to have to run five of them."

In the entire colony, Piya had found only one other print book: a copy of the Sva, the sacred text of the Tishkani state religion. Tolva opened it on his desk for an hour every morning, after which he stored it in a locked drawer in his desk. He made such a show of studying it for that hour, however, that Piya long ago concluded he'd never actually read it.

The alien book differed from Tolva's ancient Sva in every way. The alien book was a slim volume, wrapped in a paper cover printed in a garish pattern superimposed with lines of white ball-and-stick figures. Piya guessed they were the aliens' writing. They looked the way the words sounded: pointed, then round, with no relationship between their shapes and sense that Piya could detect.

Words had to be written down to make books. And words had to be stolen to be understood.

"You know, Erin, if you don't want to help me with this, you can find something else to do," the short-haired alien muttered into the access panel as Piya slipped past the pair.

"Like what? Clean up that mess in the cencom? No way. I don't even know why you don't just tear the whole thing out."

Piya's long white fingers reached out and closed around the book.

"Because it works, that's why." The short-haired alien emerged from the access panel with a noise somewhere between a sigh and a grunt.

The long-haired alien looked down. "What?"

Piya slipped the book into her pocket.

"We can't get to the port controls from here. I forgot. These Eikore'es ships always installed them under the core chamber floor. Which means we need to get under there somehow," said the short-haired alien.

"How?" the long-haired alien asked.

Piya froze as both aliens looked around the room, as if searching for something. She stood directly between them and the door – a terrible place from which to go unnoticed.

The short-haired alien's eyes met hers. "You. Can you help us?"

The alien spoke Eikore'es, which surprised Piya. The alien spoke Eikore'es badly, which surprised Piya less.

"We need to get under this room," the short-haired alien continued, pointing to the floor. "Under the power core."

Piya decided she liked the short-haired alien. This alien had no idea how pronouns worked.

Piya indicated herself, then the two aliens, then pointed toward the hallway.

"What is she doing?" the long-haired alien asked.

"I think she wants us to follow her," the short-haired one said, and took a step toward Piya. Piya retreated towards the door. The aliens followed.

Satisfied the aliens could be taught, Piya continued into the hallway. They followed, still filling the air with their strange alien language.

"Why doesn't she talk?" the long-haired alien asked.

"She's a kid, Erin. Niralan children can't talk."

"Why not? It's not like we're going to tell her mom or something."

"No, I mean Niralan children *can't* talk," the short-haired one said. They don't have the ability. Like the ones we saw on the Terminus. They don't get that ability till they become adults."

"That's stupid," the long-haired alien declared as Piya stopped in front of a heavy metal door at the far end of the corridor, opposite the entry that led into the courtyard.

Piya grasped the handle and pulled. The door didn't budge.

"What if they get lost or hurt or something?" the long-haired alien continued.

The short-haired alien exhaled loudly. "Evolution isn't stupid. Or smart. It just happens."

"Seems like it would happen better if it gave kids

a way to announce if they're starving to death or being eaten by a wild animal," the long-haired alien said. "Kinda hard to grow up and have kids of your own if you're dead."

Piya tuned out the aliens for a moment as she struggled with the door. She'd never had such a problem with it before. Perhaps the excessive moisture in the tunnels below caused it to stick. She slapped the metal surface in frustration.

"Looks like she can communicate when she needs help just fine," said the short-haired alien, stepping up to join Piya beside the door.

"Hitting things isn't communication," the long-haired alien groused.

"Looks like some water got into the mechanism," the short-haired alien said, speaking Eikore'es again. The alien's accent made Piya's teeth hurt, but she understood the words, which she appreciated. Adults rarely spoke to her, and never in an attempt to share understanding.

The short-haired alien fished a tool out of a pocket, pried off the panel beside the door handle, and reached inside. A moment later the door popped open.

Piya wedged her body into the gap, pushing the door open further as the short-haired alien replaced the panel.

"You're welcome," the short-haired alien said. "My name is Cordry, by the way. That's Lang." The alien re-pocketed the screwdriver and indicated the long-haired one.

Piya looked from one to the other. Were these names or titles? The alien's grasp of Eikore'es grammar didn't extend to social niceties.

Lang waved a hand, which meant nothing to Piya. "Are all Niralans bilingual?" Lang asked in the aliens' gravel language.

"At least," Cordry said as the aliens followed Piya through the open door. "At least, all the ones I've ever met."

"So, like, two. Two Niralans are bilingual."

"Dar and Jiya both speak at least four languages I know of," Cordry said. "And I guess Niralans have like six languages of their own."

"Yeah, but do they speak all six? I mean, humans have thousands of languages and I don't know a single one except Earth Standard."

The aliens clattered down the long metal staircase behind Piya, their words crowding into the damp air, sticking to the rock walls. The staircase treads beneath their feet punctuated each sentence with a creak. In the distance, a sodium lamp flickered feebly against one wall.

Both aliens slowed their pace. Piya looked up, noting how they grasped both handrails, how they felt for each stair tread with their feet as their eyes looked ahead, unfocused. She realized: The aliens could barely see.

"We should have brought a light," Lang said.

"I think there's one in the bag," Cordry replied. "Let me get off this staircase and I'll see if I can find it."

"Twi always carries a penlight in her pocket," Lang said.

"Twi looks in people's head-holes all day," Cordry answered as Piya stopped at the bottom of the staircase. She'd moved several steps ahead of the aliens by that point, and she didn't know how well they could see in the murky half-light of the tunnels.

The aliens' sight was even worse than she'd guessed: They nearly ran into her.

"What's wrong?" Cordry asked. "Are you all right?"

The words were Eikore'es, but they made no sense, and therefore they did not merit an answer. Piya kept walking.

The aliens glanced at one another, then followed her, Cordry pulling a handheld light from the tool bag as they walked.

The light made Piya blink, but it seemed to comfort the aliens, who immediately paused to sweep it across the rock walls and floor.

"C, look at the lights," Lang said, pointing to one of the broken sodium lamps embedded in the wall. It hung askew, its shell cracked and its bulb extinguished. All along the corridor, identical lamps sported similar damage. Only a few remained lit, sputtering in the darkness like emphysemic stars.

"Weird," Cordry said. "What caused it, d'you think? An earthquake?"

"I haven't heard anyone here mention an earthquake," Lang said.

"Well, it's not exactly a template first contact subject,

is it?" Cordry asked. "'Hello, we are from Earth, have you enjoyed any seismic events lately?'"

Lang made a noise that startled Piya. But when the alien showed no obvious signs of distress, Piya turned away and resumed her walk down the corridor.

She paused before a gap in the stone wall, created by a sheet of metal that had been bent at one corner to allow for passage into the blackness beyond. To Piya's left, the stairs extended back to the surface; to her right, the passage continued for several meters before turning to the right and plunging into gloom.

"Erin, look at this," Cordry said.

Lang looked. "What the- Is that fused into the rock?"

"Yeah, it is." Cordry trained the light on the wall with one hand; the other traced the seam between the misshapen metal and the stone. "Do you have any idea how hot it had to get to do that?"

Lang touched the wall as well. "So this must be the original crash site. There's no way to generate that kind of energy unless you're tearing through atmosphere."

"We should check out the rest of these passages when we're done here," Cordry said. "Who knows what else is down here?"

"Shouldn't we let de la Cruz handle that? Seems like crawling around creepy ancient crash sites is her job," Lang said.

"Where is your sense of adventure?" Cordry asked, sweeping the light around inside the hole.

Lang shivered. "I left it upstairs."

"Well, just stay where you are," Cordry said. "This won't take a minute." The alien and the light both vanished behind the metal panel.

"It's creepy," Lang muttered into the darkness. A few scrapes and a bang from beyond the bulkhead gap answered her.

"Found it," Cordry called. "Right where we thought it'd be."

"Do you need help?" Lang asked, approaching the hole.

"You could hold the light," Cordry said. "I just need to- AUGH!"

A rattle and a bang sounded, then Cordry flew out of the hole, shaking one arm vigorously. A brown, scaly projectile the size of Piya's hand flew across the hall. Lang jumped as it sailed past.

"What is it?" Lang asked. "Did it bite you?"

"No, but it's creepy," Cordry panted.

Piya picked it up. The Pitonki called them "bazzi," or "surprise-bugs," based on their habit of inserting themselves into bedrolls, pant legs, and other warm and dark spaces. Piya guessed this one had tried to crawl into the alien's sleeve.

Bazzi were harmless except during mating season, when they swelled to twice their usual size with venom intended to dispatch rivals. Seeing no trace of the bright ultramarine hue of bazzi venom, however, Piya allowed the insect to trundle up her arm and into her braid. It would make a good addition to dinner; Piya especially liked them fried.

Cordry and Lang stared at her, eyes wide, with face shapes Piya couldn't interpret. If they'd been Tishkani, she'd have guessed they were angry – or that they were about to claim that they were. With the aliens she couldn't tell. They might not even be people.

"I guess they're not dangerous," Lang squeaked.

"I guess." Cordry bent to pick up the light.

"Are you done in there?" Lang asked.

"As done as we need to be. Why – do you still want to explore, or-"

"I'm game if you are," Lang said. "Besides, she's wearing the creepy bug as a hair ornament. If that's the worst thing down here, then it's fine."

Piya watched the aliens converse, frustration tugging at her thoughts. Even though the aliens never shut up, she was no closer now to deciphering their language than she was when they entered the core chamber. They also had the adult habit of cutting her out of conversations, including her only as an afterthought, when they wanted something.

As if confirming her thoughts, Cordry spoke in Eikore'es again. "Is it safe to go that way?" the alien asked, pointing down the corridor.

And even when they spoke a language she understood, they didn't speak it well. The word for "safe" the alien used, *miro*, implied only a lack of mortal peril. It omitted the realm of things worse than death.

The answer to the question Cordry asked was "yes," but it wasn't the question the aliens needed to ask. Piya didn't know how to tell the aliens they'd asked the wrong question – or even whether the question was wrong for the aliens. After all, perhaps the aliens couldn't experience harm from anything but physical threats. Maybe they weren't even things.

Piya walked a few steps down the corridor, then paused, knowing the aliens would follow her. They did.

"We're moving away from the compound," Lang said, consulting a flat, shiny handheld device. "Toward the river."

"That makes sense," Cordry said. "These caves were probably all carved out by the underground water flow. They might even connect to the river itself."

"We're not going to drown down here or something stupid like that, are we?"

"Of course not. We're fine as long as we stay above the level of the river." Cordry held the light so that Lang could pick her way over a mound of rubble. "Besides, Niralans can't swim either."

"Mom can. She says her dad taught her."

"Niralans don't really have fathers, Erin."

"And Jiya's not really my mom, C." Lang's tone developed a dizzy swing that made Piya listen more closely. It also made Cordry's nose wrinkle.

"I'm just saying," Cordry said.

"I know what you're saying, and it's dumb. I-"

"Erin, stop talking for a minute."

"Why should I?" Lang asked.

"I'm serious. Look at this." Cordry swept the light across the stone wall to their left.

Maybe it was the sudden increase in volume or drop

in pitch, but something in the alien's voice stopped Lang's chattering. Lang looked where Cordry pointed – down precisely the corridor the aliens hadn't asked the right questions about.

"This isn't naturally occurring," Cordry said. "Someone dug this out. Look, you can still see tool marks in the rock."

"Recently, then?" Lang asked.

"I don't know." Cordry turned to Piya. "Does anyone else live down here?" the alien asked.

The answer, of course, was no. No one lived down here. Not anymore.

"She's not going to answer you," Lang said in a sing-song voice.

Cordry asked the same wrong question as before. "Is it safe to go this way?"

Even if Piya could speak, the aliens would never believe her. Piya pushed past them and entered the tunnel.

"I guess that's a yes," Cordry said and followed Piya. Lang made a snorting sound and brought up the rear.

"We're going uphill again," Lang said as they crept along the tunnel, which was much smaller than the previous passages. Once or twice, she and Cordry both ducked their heads to avoid hitting low-hanging protrusions of rock. "And look, there's some kind of rockslide ahead."

Cordry raised the light. Lang screamed.

Before them, the path sloped downward suddenly, cut off by a massive pile of stone that filled the passage. Jutting from the bottom of the pile were the remains of a Niralan hand.

Chapter 6

Cordry recovered first. "What happened here?"

The answer lay in front of the aliens. Piya didn't know why the answer wasn't obvious, but she pointed at the rockslide and then to the hand.

"I see that," Cordry said. "How many of them were there?"

Piya, who had never learned to count beyond the tips of her own fingers, did nothing.

Cordry tried again. "Who were they?"

Piya indicated the rockslide again, drew a large circle with her hand, then indicated herself.

"Is she saying she killed them?" Lang blurted as Piya repeated the gesture.

"I think she's saying she was one of them. That they couldn't talk either." Cordry pointed to the hand, then to Piya. "They were children? Like you?"

Piya repeated the gesture.

Lang swayed on her feet. "I'm going to be sick."

Cordry swept the light away from the rock pile at once. "Come on," the alien said to Piya. "We have to get her to the surface."

The fastest way to the surface lay beyond the rockslide that blocked their path. But the second fastest way brought them out not far from the site, at an outcropping of rock several meters from the compound wall, facing the river and the Pitonki camp.

Piya led them up the steep incline and out of the cave entrance, into the sunlight. Both aliens collapsed to the ground, leaning against the rocks, gasping.

"I'll be all right," Lang said, her eyes closed as she leaned against the stone.

"You sure?" Cordry asked.

Lang moved her head up and down. "C, what do you think happened down there?"

"Natural disaster? Some kind of uprising?" Cordry's shoulders rose and fell. "I don't know. And I don't think there's anyone we can ask."

"Why not? She wouldn't have led us down there if it was off-limits, right?"

Cordry's shoulders moved again. "Maybe. But how do we even phrase that question? 'Hey, we found your secret stash of Niralan corpses, what's up with that?'"

Lang shuddered. "That's gross."

"That's my point. There are some things I don't think we can make polite conversation about. Besides-" The alien's voice dropped. "Maybe this is a good thing."

Lang scrunched up her face. "What?"

"I'm serious," Cordry said. "If they are children, like

the ones we saw on the Terminus slave floors, and they're all dead, well – they can't really be sold as slaves if they're dead."

Lang clamped both hands over her ears. "I'm not listening to this anymore."

"Fine," Cordry said. "We should tell the commander, at least."

"You can tell the commander," Lang said. "I'm staying right here till I stop feeling like I need to puke."

"I'll wait," Cordry said.

The aliens sat next to one another against the rock for several minutes. Piya found herself mildly surprised. She'd never heard these aliens stay silent for so long.

Eventually, Lang spoke again. "Can we talk about last night?"

"Do you want to talk, or do you want to yell at me some more?" Cordry's shoulders sagged. The alien began drawing patterns in the dirt with one finger.

Lang exhaled noisily. "I'm sorry, okay? I mean it. You just – weirded me out, is all."

"How so?"

Piya had begun to recognize patterns in the aliens' words to one another, yet the content of those words and the meaning of their elaborate facial pantomime continued to escape her. The tension that crackled in the air between them, however, was unmistakable. The aliens worked as a unit, but they struggled as a pair.

"Look, C, it's not that I don't like you. I do. You're fun. We're fun. It's just that I don't think I'm as serious about you as you are about me. And I don't – I don't know how to say that without being a jerk."

The alien's language reminded Piya of migrating waterfowl. Individually, the words flapped and faltered, laboring to take flight; together, they soared.

Cordry's arms crossed. "Well, you told me, anyway."

"Look, you're a great friend," Lang said, too quickly for Piya to distinguish words from one another. "I don't want to mess that up. Besides...."

Cordry repeated Lang's last word, but with a rising tone Piya couldn't interpret. "Besides?"

Lang stared into the distance "Besides...I think I'm in love with David."

Cordry yelped. Lang jumped.

"David? *Seriously?*"

"Yeah. Why?" Lang asked. "There's nothing wrong with-"

"I'm not saying there is," Cordry broke in, speaking more loudly than before. "I'm saying-"

"C, calm down. You're all red in the face. You look like-" Lang broke off, staring wide-eyed at Cordry. Cordry stared back. For a moment, their faces were mirror images of one another.

Then Lang spoke again. "Wait. Are you in love with him too?"

Silence flattened them both. Piya leaned forward for a better view. Koja would have called the scene *jhav* – improper, uncanny, even morbid – but Koja didn't need to know. Niralans only stared at one another like that when they intended either to have sex or to fight one another to the death.

Piya wondered which one the aliens would choose.

They chose neither. Instead, Cordry looked down, skin turning from pink to red.

"No," Cordry said. "It's just...I think you can do better, that's all."

Cordry looked away, as if trying to avoid a fight, but Lang leaned forward as if spoiling for one. "Better? Better how? David's risking his life for those Niralan kids on the Terminus."

"There's not *kids*, Erin."

"Well, I'm not calling them what Mom did. La'ilikai? That's cruel. My point is that when someone else needed help, David at least ran *into* the danger."

"Against orders."

La'ilikai. The first Niralan word she'd heard any of the aliens pronounce correctly was an epithet. Piya didn't know what to make of this discovery. Perhaps the aliens had as little regard for her as she did for them.

"Jiya's orders were wrong and you know it," Cordry said, rounding on Lang. "We're not – we're not *Dar*. She can't just make us do whatever's convenient for her and her people."

"Convenient? David and the rest of Sparrow Company are probably saving *lives* or something. You could have helped them, but you ran off to mess around with engines like you always do."

"Fine, I'm a coward and David is a big damn hero. You happy?"

Lang huffed. "You're not a coward. You're just jealous because David is a better engineer than you are."

The silence that followed these words felt like a warning. Piya eyed the two aliens uncertainly. Cordry and Lang were eye to eye once again, an obvious threat.

"I can't believe you'd say that," Cordry said.

"What-"

"How dare you. I can't believe you'd say that. After you wanted to be *friends-*"

"Look, I'm not saying you're bad at your job, just that you're kind of arrogant about it. Not everyone gets to go to some fancy corp academy at age 13, but that doesn't meant they can't learn stuff in the real world like-"

Cordry's face was now both red and wet. "You know what, Erin? Just shut up. Maybe it's better if you do just dump my ass."

Lang jumped to her feet. "You know what? Fine. I never wanted to come on this stupid job anyway."

Cordry stood as well. "Erin, wait." But Lang was already running toward the ship, long yellow hair streaming in the wind.

Cordry slumped back against the rock, eyes closed.

Piya sat down as well. Her hand went to the book, concealed in her pocket. She wanted to peruse it, to see if she could make any sense of the ball and stick language - the patterns that danced on the cover seemed to promise better luck in print - but she didn't want the aliens to know that she'd helped herself to their words.

To her surprise, Cordry looked at her suddenly, then indicated her pocket.

"You might as well take that," the alien said. "Erin's not going to come back for it, I guess. Not if it means talking to me."

Piya stared at the alien, then slowly withdrew her hand from her pocket.

Cordry stood, brushing dirt from the toolbag. "I guess I'm going back to work. You can get home all right by yourself, right?"

Piya pointed toward the compound.

"Right," Cordry said, and walked away, wiping away face-wetness with one sleeve. Piya watched the alien go, her mind buzzing with plans.

Piya Nahara had a book.

Hayek returned to his quarters after dinner to find Dar on his bed, her attention buried in her omnipad. Relief lapped at him like a wave at the sight of her.

He watched her as he pulled off his boots. She hadn't even looked up as he entered, engrossed in her reading – a novel, he imagined, or a book of poetry.

His smile faded as he examined her face. This was no tidy domestic scene. Dar was struggling with something.

Rather than disturb her with speech – that most foreign of territories – Hayek sat down behind her on the bed, slipping his arms around her waist. She leaned against his chest, her mind still on the omnipad. He'd read her right: beneath her quiet exterior frothed a maelstrom of confusion, tinged with anger and a profound sense of loss.

Hayek needed only a moment's glance at the screen to find the source of the storm. Dar wasn't reading at all. She was staring at a photograph of Meredith Cattrell.

Dar had lost Meredith less than two months before. Dar had lost Meredith twice: Once, Meredith's physical death in an attack on Station 32, and again a few days later, when the *Jemison*'s own medical team had stripped Dar's remaining memories of Meredith from her limbic system in order to prevent Dar dying of her own grief.

Dar Nantais and Meredith Cattrell had been married for over twenty years. Now, Dar struggled to remember Merri's name.

Hayek closed his eyes against his own sense of guilt. It stung him whenever Meredith was mentioned. Like most guilt, his had no truck with reality; Hayek hadn't been responsible for Merri's death, hadn't known her at all beyond a few terse words exchanged the one time they'd met. But he'd ended up in bed with Merri's widow only a few weeks later – if it had even been that long.

Yet the guilt didn't plague him most. What hurt far worse was the knowledge that while Dar did not remember Merri, Hayek did.

A chance contact with Dar's limbic fluids pre-erasure had given Hayek a heartbreaking obsession with Dar and a heartbroken access to her most recent memories. Hayek remembered Merri as Dar has known her;

now, he was the only one who knew exactly what she had lost.

"Do you want to talk about it?" he asked.

"We've been thinking. About Piya Nahara," Dar said. Even in the silence of his quarters, his chin resting on top of her head, Hayek had to strain to hear her voice.

She hadn't finished, so he said nothing.

A moment later she added, "This woman, in the photo. She's...important to that question, somehow. Of children."

Hayek took a deep breath, let it out.

"Do you remember why?" he said.

"No. She's...." Dar ran a finger over Merri's smiling face. "She's supposed to be here. I just can't remember *why*."

It was the closest he'd come to crying since Koshka.

"She was your wife," Hayek said, repeating a conversation they'd had several times already, one he knew they'd have several times more, until the chasm in Dar's psyche left by the loss of Merri healed over at last. If it ever did. If it ever could.

"We lost her in an attack on Station 32," he continued. "You were here, on the *Jemison* – you helped us save the ship."

"She's supposed to be here," Dar said, with the stubbornness of a child.

She is. And I'm not. "Are you worried about Piya's amaron?" he asked.

"We have no consent on that," Dar said. *La'siton*: In Niralanes, it had the force of an epithet.

Still, it wasn't a *no*. "Are you working on it?"

"Koa hasn't replied to my message," Dar said.

"That's not surprising, out here."

"She was human," Dar said.

Her attention had returned to the photograph. Hayek pressed a kiss to the top of her head. "Yes, she was."

"How would she have known what to say?"

"You knew each other nearly your entire adult lives," Hayek said. "If anyone would have known you after all that time, it was her." *And I'd give anything to know you half as well*, he added privately.

Dar shook her head, then deactivated the omnipad's screen. "Bathroom," she said, sliding free of his arms.

Hayek let her go and picked up the pad, studying the image: Auburn-haired Meredith, looking years younger than he remembered her, and Dar, who didn't seem to have aged a day. They stood on a pier overlooking a sparkling blue expanse of water. Merri's smile beamed from the screen; in Dar's eyes, Hayek swore he saw joy.

A popnote interrupted his thoughts: *Incoming mail: Nantais, Koa.*

Hayek glanced briefly in the direction of the bathroom, then swiped the note.

To: Dar Nantais, ISS *Jemison*
From: Koa Nantais, Ambassador

This response is later than I would have liked it to be, and while I'd like to blame that on certain diplomatic tensions I mediated recently, the truth is I haven't known how to reply.

First: Amaron is, as you know, necessary for Nirala's survival.

Second: That survival is in the aggregate.

Third: As her survival has also depended upon our willingness to lead granular lives, I hesitate to lay that aggregate responsibility on any particular instant.

Fourth: If Eri Nereved had not made the choice to stand for us, you and I would be in the same position to which you consider condemning Piya Nahara.

(Anev reminds me to remind you that her name is no excuse for your neglect. As if I didn't know what it is to be Nahara.)

Fourth, With a Caveat: If you have found what we think you've found, silence might be a mercy. Or a curse. "What does the survival of Nirala demand?" is not a question we should have to answer alone, but it has become one.

Fifth: Of course you have to lie to

the child about what a speaking, emergent adulthood entails. *Lili Amarones* allows you to do nothing else.

Fifth, With a Caveat: I have long believed there must be another way to raise our children. Nirala was not always burdened with reading; we have done this differently. And if Jiya did nothing else worthwhile, she did equip you to solve that problem. Piya Nahara could be exactly who you need to execute the solution.

Start with that book I sent you. It's the sort of tool you'd find useful in this situation — because of its diversion from *Lili Amarones*, not in spite of it. I know paper is archaic, but this one needs to be touched.

Isshai Nirala.

Koa

Hayek frowned. He hadn't expected a clear answer from Koa. He'd never met her, but from Dar's and Molloy's descriptions Hayek had deduced that Koa Nantais was basically one damn thing after another.

Besides, every interaction he'd had with Niralans so far had taught him that obfuscation came as naturally to them as breathing. Even their language was constructed to elude, a series of tunnels leading to dead ends.

Nevertheless, he believed he understood at least a few of the implications Koa had made – implications that disturbed him. *If you have found what we think you've found, silence might be a mercy.* Was Koa suggesting that allowing the Niralans on Viokaron to go extinct might be not only acceptable but a net benefit to Nirala? When so few Niralans had survived the Second Empire to begin with?

Koa's repeated references to "the survival of Nirala" – *Nirala von* – bothered him as well. He knew Dar's best-kept secret: She was La'Isshai, one of the handful of Niralans tasked with protecting their home world from harm, equipped with both the fighting skills and the will to harm that made the La'Isshai a persistent threat to the rest of their kind.

Dar had already deduced the Niralans on Viokaron were La'Isshai as well, which already made Hayek hesitant to trust her around them. He'd seen what happened when Dar lost control. He'd shot her for it – perversely, the one thing he'd done to date that had increased her trust in him.

Was Koa suggesting that Dar try to "raise" Piya – *whatever that means to them* – as some new kind of La'Isshai, a next-generation assassin or spy? Or was she suggesting the opposite, that Dar abandon Piya, Ola, and Koja altogether? Hayek couldn't say he liked either option.

He heard the shower shut off and deactivated Dar's omnipad with a tap, a pang of guilt hitting him as he did. She'd talk about it or she wouldn't – probably the latter – but he had no business reading her mail in the first place.

Molloy's voice in his ear made him jump. "Molloy to Hayek."

"Hayek here," he said automatically, realizing as he did that the captain hadn't caught him reading Dar's mail. She'd tagged him through the comms.

"I need you in the lower cargo bay," Molloy said. "Bring Nantais. And pack a bag. Both of you."

Chapter 7

It wasn't that Hayek minded camping. He'd never actually camped, but he'd slept outdoors often enough during his vagrant teenage years to understand the concept.

What Hayek minded was Molloy's sudden order to pack a bag and head down to the Pitonki camp, when he had been looking forward to a quiet evening in his own (warm) quarters, to a hot meal and a book. In short, the opposite of what he was doing now, which was lugging a pack and a shelter kit across the rapidly-dimming taiga toward a constellation of small fires that flickered in the distance.

But he hadn't complained, because Molloy was right: the crew needed him. The Pitonki had graciously invited the research team to stay on site. The research team had joyfully accepted. And none of the *Jemison*'s crew had yet learned their way around Pitonk'ol like Hayek had.

After several hours with them, he'd managed to acquire enough of their language to muddle through without the translator, though he still consulted it occasionally. He was beginning to like Pitonk'ol. Its structures reminded him of Japanese, and there was a lilt to the vowels he'd always felt belonged in other Viidan languages but had never found there.

He was beginning to like the Pitonki, too, in spite of himself. Unfailing optimism was a trait he tended to dislike in humans; it spoke to him of an outlook born of the expectation, learned in childhood, that the world was essentially fair and safe and could be reasonably counted on to stay that way. He'd never seen the world that way himself. He'd never had the chance.

Pitonki optimism was different. It was quieter, more contained; these were a people who knew how harsh the world could be, but had, somehow, not let it harshen them. Hayek had the distinct impression that the Pitonki scientists had agreed to work with his team mostly for the opportunity to exercise hospitality toward someone who might appreciate it. He also had the distinct impression that Tolva and his cohort didn't think much of Pitonki hospitality.

Let them. He liked it fine.

Molloy hadn't said why she was sending Dar out with him. Dar didn't ask, and Hayek didn't care: despite the tension of the previous night, he'd rather fall asleep beside her than anyplace else in the world.

The research team had set up camp alongside the Pitonki bivouac, surrounding a large central campfire and common area. Rain de la Cruz, the ship's anthropologist, met them near the edge of the camp. She had the energy of three people on an ordinary day, but here, in the midst of a people she had never met and had been reliably informed were extinct, de la Cruz was vibrating with excitement.

"We made space for you over here, commander," de la Cruz said. "Commanders. Do you want help setting up?"

Hayek hesitated. He'd never actually set up a tent before, nor had he ever been ashamed of that fact. But admitting it in front of two career IS officers—both of whom had "roughed it" in several different types of terrain as part of their training—bothered him. Especially when one of them was Dar.

"Yes, please," Dar said, to Hayek's immense relief.

Not that she was the one who needed help, he thought as he watched Dar and de la Cruz set up their tent. Out here, Dar seemed more comfortable than he had ever seen her, moving deftly through the tangle of equipment and communicating by means of a few quiet, confident orders.

But then, Interstellar Science *was* her career, in a way that it had never been Hayek's. He still tended to think of Dar Nantais as a vagrant they'd picked up for her skill with computer languages. Until now, he'd never given serious thought to the fact that she, in fact, understood IS better than he did. Her mother was a career officer; Jiya, if she were anything like most careers, had probably started planning her daughter's tenure with Interstellar Science before Dar could walk. Dar's schools would have been chosen with an eye to service; she would have walked straight out of college and into the officers' training program. She was Jiya Nantais's daughter and Mai Nantais's granddaughter: with that pedigree, only the grossest incompetence could have killed her career.

And she wasn't incompetent. Dar was, in fact, good at her job. Better than Hayek was at his, anyway. Hayek had gone from doing sketchy odd jobs on Mars to first officer of the *Jemison* in less than a week, based solely on Molloy's instincts and a three-minute conversation. Fourteen years later, he still didn't understand what his captain saw in him.

He shook his head to clear it as one of the Pitonki approached him: Denavra, the group's leader and his primary guide to their world – a world Hayek had not expected to be welcomed into so readily. Denavra and her people were the friendliest Viidans Hayek had ever met.

They were also the smallest Viidans Hayek had ever met: Denavra stood eye to eye with him, minus the mane.

"You brought your Niralan," Denavra said, and Hayek recalled something else he appreciated about the Pitonki: They had no use for small talk.

Nor had he missed her choice of *your*: Ehel, as in "your beloved," not as in "your subordinate," "your colleague," or even "your confidante."

Guess I'm that obvious. "I did."

"I'd like to speak to her," Denavra said. "To both of you."

As if sensing her presence was desired, Dar emerged from the tent as Denavra spoke. Hayek waved her over and she joined them, bare-armed in the chill breeze sweeping across the snow. He shivered in spite of himself. It was like she didn't even feel the cold.

"Denavra, Dar Nantais, our computational linguist," he said in Pitonki, for Denavra's benefit. "Dar, this is Denavra, their leader – insofar as they have one."

His gaze flicked from one to the other as he spoke. Hayek had grown up around Viidans; he'd learned to read their body language the same way he'd learned Tish Kan, automatically. (It had always frustrated him that he hadn't been able to learn human body language so easily.)

Most Viidans bristled to some degree in the presence of Niralans, and vice versa. But the way Dar tilted her head to the right, the way Denavra's eyes followed the motion, told Hayek that neither woman was having a run of the mill reaction to the other.

Denavra's next words surprised him nonetheless. "Piya Nahara is the only child left on this planet. She shouldn't be."

Their meaning didn't startle him; Dar had been saying the same thing for days. Their cadence, the *sound* of them, was all wrong. It was as if someone had put Tish Kan and Niralanes in a blender.

He didn't realize he'd looked to Dar for confirmation until she turned to him.

"Eikore'es," she said.

In the manner of the Empire: The pidgin formed during the Second Empire, which no one had spoken for centuries and which Hayek couldn't seem to escape, not in space and not here. The Pitonki, it seemed, remembered it.

So did the La'Isshai.

"That's why we're here," Dar said. Or what Hayek heard, at least.

"She hasn't been the only one for long. We estimate they've shipped hundreds of your children away from here over the years," Denavra said.

Hundreds. The word dizzied Hayek; he didn't bother to calculate what it worked out to in base-10. More Niralan children than existed anywhere else in registered space, he knew that.

"Where do they go?" Dar asked.

"That I don't know," Denavra replied. "Let me be clear. I do not have direct evidence that your children are in fact being shipped off the planet.

"What I have are ever-dwindling numbers of the silent ones, the disappearance of whom coincides with the departure of various supply ships from the compound, at predictable intervals throughout the year. Without a clear count of how many of you there are, we cannot guess at how quickly the population is decreasing. And – forgive me – you all look damnably alike."

Hayek stifled a smile.

"When is the next supply ship due?" Dar asked.

"Not for several months."

Hayek didn't have to touch her to know what she was thinking: *Then confronting them is out of the question.* The fact relieved him; he guessed it relieved her as well. Dar preferred the subtle approach when she had a choice.

"Where do they come from?" Dar asked. "The children."

"From the compound," Denavra said, as if the answer wasn't obvious. "Most of it is underground – more, I'll predict, than you've seen. The area we're set up in now sits atop a series of underground caves. We spend winters in them. They connect to the compound's substructure, though the path is treacherous."

"Can I get into the compound from this side, then?" Dar asked.

Denavra indicated the answer was no. "The only safe route caved in last spring. If you intend to find a way in, it'll have to be from the compound side – which rather defeats the purpose, since your goal is to enter the compound itself. I don't envy you the task."

"Why are you telling me this?" Dar asked.

Denavra gazed past her, into the distance. Toward the compound.

"We are not fighters," she said at last. "If I could devise a way to free your children without resorting to force, I would do so without hesitation. But there is a legacy of military training among the compound-dwellers that we lack."

She's not kidding, thought Hayek. Viidans were notorious among sentient species for their ferocity; the Tishkani were notorious among Viidans.

"And – I think – among your children, something even more dangerous," Denavra added. Dar did not respond.

Nevertheless, Denavra observed her for a moment, as if Dar were a puzzle whose pieces had just clicked into place. "Either way, the risk is great. Not least because I understand we are all that remains of the Pitonki."

"Yes," said Dar.

Denavra took a long, measured breath. "More than anything," she said, "I tell you because just as only an amaie can make another amaie, only one of Nirala's children can confront another,"

Dar frowned – a human expression, Hayek noted, and meaningless to the Viidan. "Forgive me–"

"Your children," Denavra said gently, "are being sold by Ola Nahara."

Hayek looked at Dar, certain he hadn't heard Denavra correctly. Certain Dar would be as shocked as he was if he had.

Yet Dar had heard the same thing he had, and he could only describe her as *grim*.

"We'd hoped for an alternate explanation," Dar said, and Hayek realized she had anticipated this news all along. He'd been so preoccupied with her reaction to Tolva that he hadn't seen how fiercely she'd set herself against the Niralan elder.

"Hoped," Denavra echoed. Hayek had heard it too: *Hada*, to hope without expectation or chance of fulfillment.

"You can't be serious," Hayek said, his first contribution to the conversation since it began, and a pathetic one. But he couldn't let Denavra's words pass unnoticed.

"Again, I have no direct evidence," Denavra said. "I do have Ola Nahara's continuous and persistent presence with these ships and their masters, at every landing, for years. She spends time aboard those ships. She makes their decisions. Whether she has help from anyone else in the compound I cannot say, but what I know draws me inevitably to the conclusion that nothing passes out of this world without her involvement."

"But...why?"

Dar shook her head – another human gesture. In a different world he might have teased her for it.

"We'll see," she said, a response sufficiently human – and meaningless – to grate on him.

Denavra seemed to share his frustration. "Whatever you do, do it gently," Denavra said. "I know what you are." Even with her slight build and choice of words, Denavra made this statement sound like a threat.

"There are too few of us left for violence," Dar said, and walked away without further comment. Only by looking past her, along her path of travel, did Hayek realize that Dar hadn't been staring at nothing for the last several conversational exchanges: She had seen Koja Nantais approaching the Pitonki camp in the gathering darkness.

Denavra caught his eye, and Hayek shrugged. "I don't know what to do with her either."

To his surprise, the Pitonki leader laughed.

"That's easily solved," she said, displaying the same levity that had appealed to him in the first place. "If you need help, my tent is open. To both of you."

It took Hayek a moment to realize what she'd said. By the time the embarrassment hit him, Denavra had walked away.

He stood in the darkness for a moment, his face on fire, grateful that the Pitonki didn't believe in parting pleasantries either.

The rest of the *Jemison*'s team had been drawn into a Pitonki game called "chorps," which Hayek thought of as a cross between baseball and hopscotch and at which he sensed he'd be genuinely terrible. Rather than join them, he took a seat beside one of the campfires and stared into the flames as his head spun.

Where to begin? Everything he knew, or thought he knew, about their mission on Viokaron had been disjointed.

Fragments swirled in his head like leaves in a storm drain. The cages in rows on the vast floors of the Terminus. Their occupants silent, dead-eyed. *La'ilikai*: Not even things.

Denavra's voice: *Your children are being sold by Ola Nahara.*

No, he said to himself, recalling the other set of eyes he'd seen on the Terminus's auction floor, the cold sadistic stare belonging to someone who radiated all the presence those caged Niralans had lacked: Aqharan Bereth, the head of the United Governments of Riyal.

Jiya Nantais blamed him for the slave trade. Hayek knew in his bones she was right. No one piqued his sense of danger that sharply unless he was a threat.

*But...*his mind whispered, and Dar's resignation

sprang into focus.

Hadaai hadaes, she'd said: to hope without possibility of fulfillment. Without touching her, Hayek had known which of her various feelings she'd meant. It was the one that filled her limbs like miasma when she thought of her mother.

Jiya. Jiya, who had pointed them at Aqharan Bereth. Jiya, who had stolen an entire ship from under her former commanding officer – not once, but twice. Jiya, whose control over Dar reached the level of myth, or religion. Jiya, who had sent them here.

What if she-

Hayek clamped down on that thought before it emerged. Jiya Nantais had nothing to gain by getting her daughter killed.

Did she?

Dar's mother wasn't a problem he could deal with now. He pushed her out of his mind and focused again on Viokaron, on the problem in front of them now.

Tolva. Tolva had a colony to run, and Tishkani were known for two things: A ruthless imperialist doctrine and a puritanical hatred of vice.

Tish Kan had run the occupation of Nirala during the Second Empire. Their primary cultural values made them ideal candidates, then and now. Most Viidans had come to accept the continued existence of Niralans in the universe; the Tishkani, even now, still firmly believed the species ought to be stamped out.

And as much as he loved Dar – as much as he hated himself for thinking it – Hayek couldn't completely disagree with them.

He'd dealt with addiction most of his life. One of the best things Molloy had ever done for him was to put him on a ship where substance use wasn't merely disallowed but actively disliked. His captain had been an addict herself; she understood the work it took.

He'd told Molloy, several weeks ago, that his feelings for Dar weren't an addiction. Yet he knew, to some extent, they were. His entire relationship with her relied on the fact that his brain no longer functioned in the same way without the compounds built into her limbic system.

For humans, the connection was temporary, the damage minimal. He'd never develop a tolerance; losing her would be uncomfortable, but not fatal.

Viidans had no such luck.

The Second Empire's answer to *has evenen Niraldi* – the Niralan question – had had several prongs: Population control, outright discrimination, extrajudicial murder. It had stopped short of simply wiping the species from existence. Then, and now, there were Tishkani who believed that failing to eliminate Nirala had been a mistake.

That any Tishkani would have allowed Niralans to go on living in their colony surprised Hayek. It also reminded him that he'd never asked what, exactly, Denavra and the Pitonki's relationship to the colony's Niralans were.

The most logical explanation for Tolva's continued tolerance of Ola, Koja, and Piya's presence was that it benefited him and the colony. Natural resources were sparse on Viokaron, and Hayek doubted Tolva – or any Tishkani in his position – would hesitate to sell whatever resource he had, especially if that resource was Niralans.

Even if that resource is La'Isshai?

Maybe, he answered himself. *What if not letting them speak prevents them from....* He didn't need to finish articulating that thought; his memory of Dar standing over Molloy, blade in hand, sufficed.

He recalled his qualms while reading Koa's letter to Dar, his suspicion that Koa had asked Dar not only to bring Piya into a speaking adulthood but, by so doing, to give her some power, some ability that La'Isshai like Dar and Koa did not possess.

Hayek had never met Koa, who was Dar's cousin and, he suspected, the one great lost love of Molloy's life. Her name, in Niralanes, meant "compassion." Molloy's and Dar's descriptions of her had never given Hayek reason to think she didn't live up to the description.

Until now. Now he didn't know who to distrust most: Jiya, Tolva, or Koa.

But if Tolva needs to trade them for something, why is he letting that resource run out?

Niralans made poor livestock, even mute. They typically reproduced at a rate barely sufficient to sustain their own population. Most had only one child in a lifetime; two was unusual, three nearly unthinkable.

To further complicate the problem, Niralans reproduced by parthenogenesis. Breeding Niralans – causing them to reproduce without their willing participation – was impossible. As far as he knew.

It's why you'll never be a father, whispered his self-loathing.

He closed his eyes. It rarely did him any good to fight this particular demon. Hayek spent a good deal of his career assessing threats. In fact, he had always been his own worst enemy.

The snow crunched behind him. He opened his eyes.

It was Piya, holding the book and looking at him expectantly.

"Yae?" he asked her.

She held the book out to him and jabbed at the page with one four-jointed finger.

He knew *the book*. Everyone on the ship knew *the book*. Hayek had picked it up from Dar's desk before she'd added it to the ship's library; once the crew had gotten their hands on it, his only regret had been that he hadn't finished reading it first.

Teaching Languagings to: Nonverbal Thinkers, read the subtitle, which was what had prompted Hayek to pick it up in the first place. Language was his stock in trade, but it had never been the world in which his own mind moved.

Piya jabbed the page again.

"She wants you to read to her," de la Cruz called to him from across the fire pit.

Hayek looked up. He could just make out the exoanthropologist's face, pink-cheeked from the cold, raising an eyebrow in obvious amusement.

"How can you tell?" he asked.

She smiled. "I just read her the first half. Gave me an excuse to scan it."

"She doesn't understand Earth Standard," Hayek said.

De la Cruz's smile widened into a grin. "She will by the time she finishes that book."

He took the book from Piya, who seated herself at once on the log beside him.

"Start here?" he asked her, pointing to the right-hand page. "Ao ami?"

Piya pointed to the same page.

One of Hayek's minor courses had been a workshop in dramatic storytelling, and while he hadn't thought about the class itself in nearly twenty years, the habits he'd picked up there had never fully abandoned him, either. He began:

"*Since our sense of communication rides alongside our generally elevated level of sensory information,*

you cannot be surprised if our communication

happens along all our senses at once,

expressing our emotion in movements

accompanied by shouts of joy

or screams

depending on the reception to our ways

that is always painted on your face.

The microexpressions in our faces might be invisible to strangers

but it's not because we don't make them,

it's because...."

"Commander," Dar's voice interrupted.

He looked up, first at Dar and then across the fire ring in the direction she indicated. He had the same moment of unreality he'd had the previous day before he realized he was looking, not at Dar again, but at Koja.

Koja, however, was looking at Piya. "Amiie, yaeya," she said. *Child, come with me.*

"They're reading," Dar said.

"It's halfway to sunrise," Koja replied, and Hayek blinked again; Koja's voice, like her face, was identical to Dar's.

Suddenly, selfishly, he was glad so few Niralans lived on this planet, whatever their fate they were meeting off it. Hayek was bad enough with human faces, and he blanched to imagine Dar's reaction if he repeatedly mistook her various family members for her.

Piya tugged Hayek's sleeve and pointed to the book again.

Hayek let his gaze trail over the page. *You cannot be surprised if communication/happens along all our senses at once,/expressing our emotion in movements...* He could relate. Once upon a time he had thought of himself as a metalinguistic synesthetic outcast, wired just differently enough from the rest of his species to make them inaccessible to him. Then he'd met Dar, and he'd learned exactly what it meant to wear language as a straitjacket.

The microexpressions in our faces might be invisible to strangers

but it's not because we don't make them...

Hayek flipped the book closed and looked at the title

again. *The US Book*. Who else in the universe better understood what it meant to be an *us* than Niralans?

Who else needed a way to put that state of existence into language?

He handed the book back to Piya. "Don't lose this, kid. It's important. Aopa la'fara," he repeated, in case she still didn't understand him.

Piya took the book and slipped it into her pocket.

"Amiie," Koja said again.

Piya walked out of the circle of firelight and disappeared into the darkness of the taiga. Dar reappeared a moment later, taking a seat on the log beside him.

Hayek reached for her hand: Weariness, and a sense of shelved resolve.

He'd intended to ask her, "What's on your mind?" At the touch of her fingers, he amended this comment to "You need sleep."

"In a moment," she replied.

"What do you think?" he asked. "About what Denavra said."

Her hand told him the answer before her words did. "We don't want to believe her, yet we do."

"What does this mean?" he asked.

Dar hesitated, staring into the fire, its flames reflected in her eyes. "We don't simply confront the dorie," she said.

"Seems like now would be the time to make an exception."

Dar shook her head. "It's not a matter of manners. *Olimeronai dorieeya ji.*"

Discipline proceeds from the elders. Hayek pictured the way Dar had, on the Terminus, gone from contradicting nearly everything her mother said to allying with her, the moment Jiya took her hand. Discipline didn't merely "proceed from" Niralan elders to the younger generations; the elders had, somehow, the power to force their daughters to comply.

"There has to be a way," he said.

"We'll find it."

He yawned. "Sleep first?"

"Go on," she said. "We need to think."

Hayek glanced around, then kissed her cheek. "Goodnight, Dar."

"Goodnight."

Not only had she set up their tent, he discovered as his eyes adjusted to the darkness on the far side of the campfire, but she'd also set up their cots, laid out their sleeping bags, and stowed their respective packs beneath each one. Hayek reminded himself to thank her as he kicked off his boots. He was asleep seconds after his head hit the pillow.

He awoke with a start out of a dead sleep a few hours later and lay still, eyes wide, heart racing as he regained his bearings.

In the wan light filtering through the tent walls, he could only just make out Dar's cot. He extended a hand, touching her sleeping bag to confirm his suspicions: she wasn't there. Her cot was empty, her bedding undisturbed.

That frightened him. He sat up at once, kicking his

own sleeping bag away and fumbling for his boots.

Only one of the planet's two moons was visible, but its light was sufficient for Hayek to discern that no one was moving in the camp. He made a loop of his team's tents just in case, peering hard into the shadows between them as his eyesight adjusted. Nothing.

The central fire had burned down to a few glowing embers; the smaller fires between the Pitonki shelters were dark. He circled through their shelters in the same way, hesitant to call Dar's name for fear of waking the entire camp but ever watchful for the smallest movement.

No one was stirring on the Pitonki side, either, and in fighting his growing sense of panic, Hayek nearly missed the clue: a trail of footprints, small enough to be Dar's and headed toward the compound.

Hayek followed it at once.

Away from the camp, he found it easier to see. There were few obstructions on his path, no trees or structures to block his view. He quickened his pace, following the footprints.

The compound walls rose above him a short distance away, and he hesitated; even from here, he could tell the gates were closed. How did she get in?

But the trail, he saw a moment later, did not lead to the gate. Instead the footprints curved away from the compound walls and toward a small round building that huddled beside the west wall: the Niralans' house.

Hayek followed the footprints.

They stopped at the rear wall of the hut. The wall

was built of jagged, irregular stone. Above him, on the roof, a patch near the edge had been scraped clean of snow and ice—almost as if someone had grabbed the edge and slithered over it.

Hayek found a couple of handholds and hauled himself up.

There were no footprints on the roof. Sun and wind had scoured the tiles clean, leaving only a few patches of ice.

Nonetheless, he could predict where she had gone. At the far edge of the rooftop he could see the roof of a small metal shed.

He picked his way to the edge of the roof. A gap about two and a half meters wide loomed between the two buildings—not too big to jump, but big enough that he wished he didn't have to.

Hayek backed up a few paces and charged.

His feet slipped from under him as he hit the rooftop and he landed hard on his shoulder with a thud that rattled him. He froze, listening hard, ignoring the ache in his arm and his scraped elbow. Someone had to have heard that.

The seconds ticked by. His heart ticked faster. Yet, strain as he might, he heard nothing but the sound of his own breath.

After several interminable moments he stood, expecting to hear a shout or perhaps a shot, but there was nothing.

He made his way across the roof, stepping carefully around the patches of ice. This gap, between the roof and the compound wall, was smaller than the last: narrow enough that he could use the roof edge to jump, allowing him to grab the edge of the wall.

Better get it right the first time, though, or I'll break an ankle.

Hayek rubbed his palms together briefly, braced himself, and jumped.

He hadn't even straightened his knees from the landing when he heard the unmistakable click of a Viidan sidearm in his right ear and a single barked command. "Gesseld." *Freeze.*

He froze. The language was Tish Kan, and he recognized the voice. He also recognized the tense. Only Tishkani military officers used *-eld* in the imperative.

He'd sorely underestimated Tolva.

He translated Tolva's next commands mentally, though he didn't need to; he'd been fluent in Tish Kan since he was five. *Stand up. Tell me what you're doing here.* The translation kept him calm; it kept him in control.

He let his mental voice translate his own words as well as he spoke, matching Tolva's pace and tone, though not his grammar. *I'm looking for my computational linguist. I believe she's here.*

Tolva lowered his weapon. Hayek eyed him warily.

The Viidan's next words were more welcome than any Hayek had had in his head all day. *I'll take you to her.*

He allowed himself a silent sigh of relief as he followed Tolva into the main building, across the central atrium, and down a flight of stairs. He regretted it the moment he reached the bottom.

Dar was dead.

Chapter 8

Hayek had forgotten how to breathe.

Dar's body lay half in, half out of the doorway to a glass-fronted room opposite the bottom of the staircase, her neck twisted at an impossible angle. Her long black hair pooled around her head; a few strands fell across her eyes, half-closed as if she had merely succumbed to a moment of drowsiness.

But it wasn't her face that arrested him at the bottom of the stairs or that squeezed the air from his lungs. Nor was it the shattered glass from the now-empty doorway, scattered about the floor like snow, crunching underfoot. It was the blood: filling the doorway, splashed against the glass, staining her arms and face a viscous royal blue. More blood that he knew she had; more blood than he could have imagined her body could hold.

He had no words. He had no thoughts. He couldn't *breathe*.

"Commander," a voice said from behind him.

He turned his head, unseeing even as the voice registered, even as his mind, devoid of sense, managed to dredge up two words: *imagining things.*

At first he couldn't see who had spoken: the only shape that registered as a person was a Viidan guard, clutching a rifle and scowling more from fear than toughness. But the voice had not been Viidan.

His heart sank. Of course he was imagining things. Of course he was.

Then his eye caught movement beneath the staircase, and he shifted slightly to his left, peering into the space beneath the treads, against the rock wall.

She was alive.

Dar's shoulders sagged as if she were tired, and her braid had begun to come loose. She sat on the floor, her arms pinned awkwardly behind her and fastened to one of the staircase posts by a short length of chain.

He fought for breath again. *Imagining things.*

A bruise darkened her cheek, and she held her jaw in a way that suggested she'd broken at least one tooth as well. But she was wearing the same tank top and faded jeans she'd been wearing that evening.

Her eyes met his, briefly: those eyes he loved, though he could so rarely stand to look straight into them. Her eyes.

He looked back at the body in the doorway, then back at Dar. All at once he understood.

Dar wasn't dead. Koja was. But Dar, *his* Dar, was very much alive.

And if she hadn't been chained to the staircase at that moment, he would have throttled her himself.

He got to his feet.

"Explain," he ground out. The Viidan snapped to attention.

Dar didn't look up. "I'd rather speak to the captain."

He didn't give a godsdamned what she'd rather, but she had a point. Molloy could get them out of this if anyone could.

He pulled his communicator from his jacket and contacted the ship.

"Lin here," a drowsy voice said a moment later. He made a mental note to kick the kid's ass for sleeping on the job.

"Get me the captain," he snapped.

There was a pause that made him want to yell into the communicator, then Lin said, "Hang on."

"Molloy," the captain's voice said immediately, sounding far more alert than Lin had.

"We've got a situation," he said. "Koja Nantais is dead. Commander Nantais is...implicated. Meet us in the main building."

Molloy asked no questions. He appreciated that. "On my way."

Hayek relayed the gist of this conversation to Tolva as he stuffed his communicator back into his pocket. Tolva motioned to the guard.

"Berest rach," the guard protested at once, shooting a fearful look at Dar.

Hayek thought this was a foolish thing to say to a superior officer, particularly when that officer was a seven foot tall Viidan with a gun. Stepping forward, he motioned for the guard's keys with one hand and hauled Dar to her feet with the other.

He'd been looking for an excuse to touch her anyway. He wanted to know how she felt. Whether she was afraid; whether she was hiding something from him.

She was neither, as near as he could tell, but the knowledge didn't bring him the relief he'd anticipated. Her inner world was too quiet to account for her dead doppelganger just down the hall. Why?

The guard viewed him with something like awe, which Hayek ignored. He had no reason to think Dar would try to hurt any of them, not after she'd asked for the captain. Molloy had been the only one to successfully talk her down last time.

Almost.

Hayek suddenly realized what he was seeing: Not Dar, not the rock surrounding them or the treads of the staircase as he climbed, pushing her ahead of him. The material world didn't register to him. His mind's eye saw Engineering, hissing pipes and broken consoles, and other bodies. Molloy, backed up to a wall, her hands raised; Dar, his Dar and yet not his, blade in hand.

He shook his head to clear it. This wasn't Engineering. He couldn't convict her on sight; doing so was tantamount to admitting he ought to hand her over to whatever passed for justice in this colony, and that he would not do. Whatever she had done, he would deal with it.

He loved her that much.

They entered Tolva's office. Hayek sat Dar down on one of the curved couches, a bit harder than he intended to, and sat beside her. The guard stationed himself nervously beside the door.

He said nothing as they waited for the captain, but he didn't let go of her arm, either.

Molloy entered a few minutes later, alert and tense in the way only a person dragged out of a dead sleep can be. She glanced at Hayek, then sat down at once on the edge of the round table, directly in front of Dar.

"Tell me what happened," she said.

"I found her," Dar began.

Molloy held up a hand. "Back up a bit."

Dar hesitated, then started again. "The commander and I left the ship and proceeded to the campsite, where we-"

"Start from when I went to bed," Hayek said. Molloy glanced at him, raising an eyebrow in an expression he wasn't certain whether to categorize as surprise or rebuke. He took it as both: his words had come out strained, his anger obvious.

Dar looked at the captain, who nodded.

"The commander went to bed around midnight," she said. "I waited for the others to go to bed as well. Then I left the camp and entered the compound."

"How did you get in?"

"I climbed the wall," Dar said. *That's not the whole story*, Hayek thought, but he didn't elaborate.

"I went down the stairs, and when I reached the bottom, I saw her," Dar said. "Lying in the doorway, with the glass broken. The...blood."

For the first time, Hayek realized, Dar felt disturbed: he could see the tension in her face. The sense of writhing beneath his own skin where his fingers held her arm was unmistakable—and unpleasant.

"You didn't kill her," Molloy said.

"No," Dar replied.

"Then who did?"

Dar shook her head slowly.

The sound of footsteps in the hallway silenced all three of them. As the door swung open, Hayek looked up and so did Molloy, expecting to see Tolva's or Ola's face appear in the doorway.

Instead, there entered the blandest-looking human Hayek had ever seen.

It was as if AI had been tasked with generating a human from the dataset of all existing humans. Everything about the stranger was *medium*: Medium height, medium build, medium coloring, medium features, a medium amount of medium-length hair. Hayek had the odd sensation that he had never seen this person before and yet had only ever seen this person. One thing was clear to him, however: He couldn't put a name with the face.

Molloy could.

"Quincey Dillon, you son of a bitch."

Quincey Dillon held up a hand. "I hear you, captain. Kindly do not hit me again." Hayek was intrigued in spite of himself.

"Where the *hell* did you come from?" Molloy asked.

"Orbit, which is where I've spent nine of the past ten hours." The voice matched the face: medium pitch, medium tone, medium timbre, medium tempo.

"Bullshit. I'd know by now."

Dillon smiled. It was not a nice smile. "I doubt that."

"Captain?" Hayek asked. Formulating a more complex question escaped him, but he could tell by the way Molloy's fists clenched that his wisest course – to say nothing of his duty as her first officer – compelled him to intervene. Molloy disliked a lengthy and ever-growing list of people she'd met, but Hayek had never seen her loathe one before.

"This is Agent Quincey Dillon," Molloy said, not taking her eyes off the intruder. "He's Compliance."

That's why she hates him.

Hayek had never dealt with Compliance personally. He didn't know anyone who had, for the simple reason that everyone who ever had dealt with Compliance directly had also disappeared. Some disappearances were physical. Others were mental. Either way, to face Compliance was to lose something you took for granted until you no longer had it. Interstellar Science handled routine conflicts and misbehavior via its Internal Affairs department; Compliance handled larger problems, wielding a sledgehammer or a scalpel as situations demanded and answering to no one.

Hayek wondered whether Dillon was the sledgehammer or the scalpel.

His captain didn't introduce him or Dar, which Hayek understood: If Dillon was Compliance, he already knew more about them both than they did about themselves. "I have a bigger problem than you at the moment," Molloy said.

Dillon smiled again. "Nobody has a bigger problem than me, captain. Though I'm quite easily solved, if you'll calm down. I came for the book."

No human in the history of the species had ever calmed down upon being told to "calm down," and Molloy respected tradition. "The what?"

Dillon, meanwhile, had spotted Dar. "Oh, I think your CL knows," he said with a nod in Dar's direction, "even if you don't. Do you have any idea how long I've been tracking that damn thing?"

"Something over two years, eight months and three days," Dar said, as if they were discussing the weather.

Molloy rounded on her. "You knew about this?"

Dar shook her head. "That's how long we've had the book."

"Of all the things – of all the *impossible fucking things* – a scavenger might have found valuable in that wreck, nothing went missing. Except that book," Dillon said. "Do you want to explain how it ended up in your possession?"

"No," Dar said, displaying either uncommon bravery or utter madness. One did not simply say "no" to Compliance.

"Let me rephrase that," Dillon said. "*How did you get the damn book?*"

"No, let me," Molloy interrupted. Hayek wondered if insanity was catching. "I'm sure it's a very fascinating book, but it's a book. I'm trying figure out why my CL was caught on the scene of a murder this morning, so if you don't mind-"

"Oh, not at all," Dillon said. "In fact, I took care of that on my way to this charming tete-a-tete we're having."

Molloy exchanged glances with Hayek and Dar. Dar shook her head; Hayek shrugged. "The hell do you mean?"

"I mean that Tolva and Ola, while perfectly aware that their own colleague is dead, have conveniently forgotten that your colleague had anything to do with it," Dillon said.

"How-" Hayek began, and stopped, certain the answer was *Compliance*.

"I don't like complications in my work," said Dillon, "and your ship and crew are nothing but. I wasted an hour this morning just trying to get some sense out of your anthropologist. Anyway, you may interrogate me all you like once we're back aboard the Jemison."

Molloy looked at Hayek again. He read her meaning at once: *I don't like this, but we don't have a choice.*

Hayek sighed and helped Dar to her feet. "Let's go."

"Quarters," was all Molloy said to Dar as they reentered the *Jemison*. Dar obeyed without hesitation, turning left out of the lower cargo bay as Molloy, Hayek and Dillon turned right.

"You might want to send her to Medical, captain," Dillon said blandly. "That molar isn't going to root itself."

The captain looked at Dar, who nodded.

"Do I want to know how-" Molloy stopped and sighed. "No. I don't. Go get it fixed." Dar nodded again and disappeared down an adjacent corridor. There were at least three routes to Medical from the lower cargo bay; following the rest of them would have been marginally shorter, but Hayek couldn't blame Dar for not wanting to be in Compliance's presence longer than she had to be.

Molloy reached for the comm switch as they left the cargo bay. "Benby. De la Cruz. Meet me in the mess hall, stat." She didn't wait around for an answer.

Dillon, meanwhile, seemed perfectly comfortable aboard the tiny ship – too comfortable for Hayek's liking. The Jemison was a first-generation research vessel, several decades old and long since outclassed by the larger, faster, more reliable R6 and R7 classes. Her scientific equipment was state of the art; everything else was a zombie, still shambling about the universe long past the end of its predicted life.

Only a handful of R1 crews even remained, aboard the *Jemison*, the *K. Johnson* and the *Tu YouYou*, their crews forming an extended family of likeminded weirdos. Living on an R1 required a certain personality – and a certain immunity to claustrophobia.

Dillon expressed exactly none of the traits endemic to that personality. Yet he seemed perfectly at ease aboard the *Jemison*.

Hayek had no more time to ponder the mystery. Lieutenant Benby, the ship's second officer and head of sciences, stood just outside the doorway to the mess hall. He ran a hand through his salt-and-pepper hair as they approached, as if nervous, but he met Dillon's stare readily enough.

De la Cruz joined them a moment later, her face tearstained. Molloy shot Dillon another venomous look. Hayek recalled the Dillon's comments about wasting time with their anthropologist and resolved to put the man's face through a bulkhead at the first opportunity.

First Dar, now de la Cruz. He'd be damned if he'd let any outsider take apart his crew, even if he was Compliance.

Dillon occupied Molloy's usual place at the head of the meeting table. Scowling, Molloy retreated to the seat on Hayek's right, where Dar usually sat, facing de la Cruz.

Molloy didn't wait for Dillon to start the meeting. "So you came all the way out here for a book."

Her tone said she wanted a fight; Dillon merely grinned at her. "I did."

"What makes you think we have it?" Hayek asked. De la Cruz sniffled.

"The Phobos Stack," Dillon replied. "The query for the full text could have meant anything, especially coming from an anthropologist. But then we started getting queries about the book's actual contents. You all made it painfully obvious you were actually reading it – which, as I'm sure you've already realized, you cannot possibly have been doing unless you had the book itself."

"Phobos told me it didn't exist," de la Cruz said to the tabletop.

"Phobos is right," Dillon said. "It doesn't. The sooner you all get that through your heads, the better off you'll be."

Molloy frowned. "You told Dar it had disappeared from some wreck. What wreck are you talking about?"

Dillon waved a hand. "That story hasn't been told, and I predict it never will be – save, perhaps, to five or so of my closest confidants."

"If it disappeared from anywhere, it has to exist," Molloy argued.

Dillon's face displayed a perfect mix of disappointment and rage. "Let me spell it out in smaller words. The book does not exist *in this timeline*. It is a temporal artifact, created in a separate timeline, where presumably I never had to come out here and draw you a crayon diagram to explain it.

"That makes it non-compliant. I'm here to correct that." He straightened. "So where is it?"

Hayek caught Molloy's eye. Benby shook his head slightly, a blank expression on his face. De la Cruz stared at the table.

Dillon sighed. "I'll make this easy. I will conveniently manage to lose any and all paperwork referring this crew to Compliance for behavioral redirection if you will simply tell me where the book is."

"We don't have it," de la Cruz said in a tiny voice. "I told you we don't have it."

Dillon laughed. De la Cruz flinched.

"My dear, you are a terrible liar." All mirth dropped from his face. "We can change that."

De la Cruz squeaked and covered her face with her hands.

"Lieutenant?" Dillon said. "You've been awfully quiet."

Benby shrugged. "I'm afraid I can't help you," he said. "This book you're looking for doesn't exist."

Dillon snorted. "Clever."

"You told me so yourself." Benby folded his hands on the tabletop. "And even if it did, I wouldn't know where to begin looking. I've been working double shifts as it is. No time for recreational reading."

"He's right about that," Hayek said.

"Look," Dillon said. "I can engage in these useless pleasantries with you all day long, but they aren't getting us anywhere. And I really don't enjoy employing the usual Compliance tactics. They're crude, they breed resentment, and they don't result in long-term behavior changes. All they do is reduce people to things, or worse-" He shuddered. "Or worse, *therapists*."

He sat up. "I'll offer you a deal – one that doesn't require me to babysit you until you break. I understand, captain, that your son is currently serving a six-month penal sentence on a Riyali prison base called the Terminus."

Molloy nodded once.

"I can end that sentence today and arrange his safe passage off the base. All you have to do is give me the book."

Benby straightened. De la Cruz's eyes flew to Molloy.

Fuck, Hayek thought.

Molloy swallowed. "Even if I knew where it was, how

do I know you won't just 'redirect' my crew even if I handed it over?"

"I already told you I wouldn't," Dillon said.

Molloy snorted. "Right. Like you're so trustworthy."

Dillon shook his head. "I imply to you all that I'm going to torture you like insects and you cower like we've already begun, but I tell you that I won't and suddenly I'm untrustworthy? Captain, please make up your mind. Either you can take me at my word or you cannot."

He turned to the rest of the table. "Look, I'll make this very simple. Tell me where the book is and I'll return David Molloy to this ship, none the worse for his current misadventure, after which I will forget the *Jemison* and her crew exist. Continue to lie to me, and I will end your mission, your careers, and your personhood. Are we clear?"

All four of them were staring at the tabletop now.

Molloy cleared her throat. "I'll need time to locate it."

"Captain!" de la Cruz protested. The glare Molloy shot her preempted further outbursts.

Dillon shrugged. "Take all the time you need. I have nowhere else to be." He stood. A pointed stare told them all to adjourn.

Hayek tried to catch the captain as she left, but she sidestepped him. A sharp shake of her head told him what she was thinking: *Not here. Not now.*

He caught up with de la Cruz instead. "Are you all right?" he asked.

De la Cruz sniffed and wiped her face on her sleeve. "I'll be fine. He's just an asshole, is all."

"What did you tell him?"

"Nothing he could use, I guess, or he wouldn't have come onto the ship to bully us all," de la Cruz said. Her jaw jutted out. "I certainly didn't tell him about Piya. I'm not giving a child up to Compliance."

"Good call," Hayek said, mostly to forestall the fresh wave of tears that threatened to spill down de la Cruz's cheeks. He glanced toward the mess hall doors, which Dillon had just exited. "This book seems a little too important to him to be a routine temporal anomaly."

De la Cruz shook her head. "Wait till he tries his little bad-cop routine on Dar."

Hayek said nothing. He didn't find the prospect heartening. Dillon and Dar, alone in the same room – it sounded like a recipe for disaster. He'd found Dar with one dead body already; he didn't relish finding her with another one.

Chapter 9

On their return to the *Jemison*, the captain ordered Dar to go to Medical. Dar obeyed – but not right away.

Once out of sight of the rest of the crew, she made a short detour to her own quarters, picking a precision screwdriver off her desk as she walked into the bathroom.

She rinsed her mouth out, wincing, and spat a mouthful of water and bright blue blood into the sink. She dug a length of gauze out of one of the drawers and wrapped it around one finger, then leaned toward the mirror.

The tooth had already begun to re-root itself; nudging it with her thumb sent a caustic twinge through her neck and shoulders. She took a deep breath and yanked, stuffing the gauze in place as soon as the tooth popped free.

She hadn't been surprised by the guard. She'd let him charge her, and when he'd aimed the butt of his rifle at her face she offered no resistance. Swallowing half a liter of her own blood was worth having an ironclad excuse for the tooth she'd already dislodged before she was hit.

Now, having extracted the tooth in question, she rinsed it under the tap and turned it over. It took her only a moment to separate the tooth from the tiny microchip lodged in its underside.

Balancing the microchip on the flat of the screwdriver, her free hand cupped underneath, Dar returned to her desk. She transferred the chip to a dock card and slid the card into her spare omnipad.

Back in the bathroom, she rinsed her mouth out again and stuck the tooth back in her mouth. It wasn't likely to re-root now, not after she'd dislodged it twice in one night. Still, she'd been ordered to let Medical deal with it.

Makkarah Alatwi, the ship's junior physician, hadn't been awake long; she stifled a yawn as Dar walked in, and her skin was still the pale blue that indicated Devori sleepiness, not the vivid shade she'd acquire once the cobwebs cleared from her head.

"Good morning, commander," Twi said as Dar entered. Then: "Goodness!"

"It's not as bad as it looks," Dar said.

Twi indicated one of the beds. "Sit down, and I'll tell you if it's as bad as it looks. Please."

Dar sat as Twi reached into her overstuffed pocket of her lab coat.

"What happened?" the doctor asked, fishing out a handheld medical scanner and a penlight.

"Viidiari," Dar said. "His rifle disapproved of my face."

Twi gave her a hard look, but didn't press the matter. "Did you lose consciousness?"

"No."

"You've got a fractured cheekbone," Twi said. "Nothing we can't fix. Open your mouth." She swept the penlight around the inside of Dar's mouth as Dar obliged. "I'm guessing you can feel that tooth."

"Yes," Dar said.

"You're still bleeding," Twi said. She sat back. "Are you sure you didn't lose consciousness?"

"Yes."

Twi half-lifted one hand into the Devori handshape for skepticism, then let it fall. "We may be able to encourage the tooth to root itself again," she said, "but at this point, given the trauma to your face, the healthiest thing for your jaw would be to pull it out and let you grow in the new one. That will take six to eight weeks, though. Are you prepared for that?"

"We've done it before," Dar said.

"Of course you have," Twi said. "Hold still."

Dar held still, knowing that the silence wouldn't last long; Twi talked more than anyone else on the ship, even Cordry.

"So your face got in a fight with a Viidan," Twi said. "What else have I missed this morning?"

"Compliance is here," Dar said.

Twi sat back, her eyes wide. "Why?"

"They want the book."

Twi's hands made the Devori equivalent of a scowl. "I certainly hope no one gave it to them. Compliance, *indeed.* Bunch of outdated nonsense. Open, please." She went back to work on Dar's jaw, still muttering to herself.

Dar allowed herself a private victory. For seeding ideas among the crew, nothing beat the simple tactic of convincing Twi she'd thought them up herself. By lunchtime there wouldn't be a single person on the *Jemison* willing to capitulate to Dillon's demands, no matter how violently phrased.

Dillon might know Compliance. Dar knew her crew.

A quick check of the time told him not to bother leaving the mess hall. He'd scheduled himself for lunch duty that day, and it was nearly time to begin work anyway.

De la Cruz, also on the schedule, came to the same conclusion about the time; she busied herself by un-stacking the nearest pile of chairs without looking at him. Hayek got the impression she was about to start crying again.

"What do you know about Niralan funerals?" he asked.

De la Cruz sniffed. Was it a laugh? "Going right for the gossip, commander?"

He flipped a table upright with more restraint than he felt. "Koja's a Nantais. So is Dar. I'm assuming...."

De la Cruz sobered. "Of course. Sorry." She sighed. "Yes, she'll probably participate. Almost certainly. She's the closest thing Koja has to family here. Though 'family' isn't really the right word for it."

"Kiiste," Hayek supplied. "*Ihiai.*"

"Yes, that." De la Cruz grabbed another chair. "Besides, Ola Nahara won't want anything to do with Koja's memories. Not unless her only other option is to let them disappear forever."

Hayek frowned, Dar's words returning to his thoughts: *Her name is Piya Nahara.* He knew she wanted nothing to do with Piya, but she hadn't told him why and he hadn't asked.

"Some people just don't get along," de la Cruz continued. "Nantais and Nahara are those kind of people."

"So it's like a family feud thing?"

De la Cruz shrugged and reached for another stack of chairs. "I guess you could call it that. They tend to avoid each other, for reasons no one ever explains, so I have no idea if they're rational or just some kind of long-standing bigotry."

"Dar says Koa married one, though."

"And the Montagues produced a Romeo," said de la Cruz. "Besides, 'married' doesn't mean the same thing to Niralans it does to us."

He didn't want to think about what marriage did mean to them. "So she's got a reason to attend," he said instead.

De la Cruz looked up. "I see what you're getting at, commander, and no. She probably won't eat the actual corpse – I mean, Koja. Niralans stopped doing that centuries ago. It's messy and inefficient, or so I understand."

Niralans stopped doing that centuries ago implied that, at one point, corpse-eating happened – or there would have been nothing to stop. "Should I ask what they do instead?"

"They drain the deceased's limbic system and ingest its contents," de la Cruz replied. "It allows them to incorporate the deceased person's memories. It's how they maintain their history and their sense of a shared cultural past. In fact, *not* doing it is akin to banishing the deceased person from collective memory – erasing them, like they never existed."

"Surely the living remember that person," Hayek said. "Dar hasn't forgotten Koja exists in the last six hours."

"No, but their memories work differently than ours." Hayek heard the mess hall doors open behind them. "I don't really understand the biology."

"What biology don't you understand?" Twi asked.

"The Niralan alama," de la Cruz said.

"How much does it change them, having dead people's memories in their heads?" Hayek asked. "I mean, as people."

Twi flapped a hand; de la Cruz shrugged.

"Impossible to say," de la Cruz said. "I suppose it depends on the person. And the memories."

Hayek frowned. "Would Dar know who killed Koja?"

De la Cruz shook her head.

"Maybe?" Twi supplied. "Niralan memory isn't encyclopedic. Like human memory, it's reshaped by emotion and experience, as well as by conscious attempts to make meaning from recalled events. It's possible that what Dar will extract from Koja's memories won't match what happened – if Koja even saw who attacked her. It's also possible that the question will itself be traumatizing to Dar, given that it forces her to relive that attack."

Hayek nodded. He already knew that vengeance against Koja's killer wasn't on Dar's mind. The idea of hurting her further settled the last lingering question in his mind – whether he ought, for Koja's sake, to find out how she died even if it meant finding out Dar killed her.

Twi's garrulousness saved him from having to think about his own motives. "Alama's not even their most interesting ritual."

"Really? I've always thought there's not much more fascinating than a people who incorporate their ancestors' wisdom and memories firsthand after they die," said de la Cruz.

"Biologically, I mean."

Hayek recognized Twi's gossip when he heard it. He headed for the kitchen. Opening the shutters on the serving window, he began assembling ingredients, one ear still on de la Cruz and Twi's conversation.

"It shouldn't even be possible," he heard Twi say.

"I've read rumors that amaron involves setting Niralan children on fire, but I never knew what to make of them," de la Cruz said. "It's so easily understood as a metaphor. Even some human cultures use 'lighting the fire of the mind' as a way to describe teaching or learning or coming of age."

"It's not that kind of metaphor," Twi said, "but it's not entirely literal, either. At least, not usually. Too many things can go wrong when you've got an inconsistent heat source like an open flame. Their circulatory system still has to displace a great deal of heat very quickly, and it's not always up to the task.

"But they do expose children – adults, too – to a rapid and substantial increase in body temperature, which triggers rapid growth in the language centers of the brain. Also in the areas that manage what humans call the ego or sense of self."

Hayek turned on the kitchen's bioprinter, then fetched a couple mixing bowls while the machine whirred through its familiar startup sequence.

"The Alashkani explorer Ah Nengua said 'they set their children alight, and the fire draws out their souls' – *he'etera*, which was also used in First Empire Alashkani to mean 'language' or 'thought,'" he heard de la Cruz say.

"It's as good a description as any," Twi replied. "As far as I know, though, no one's ever discerned how amaron works, exactly. It's not like Niralans let outsiders get anywhere near the ritual itself, and it'd probably offend them to suggest they send their children through it wearing cortical sensors."

"If a cortical sensor can even survive that kind of heat damage."

The bioprinter beeped, and Hayek reached for its control panel. Before he touched it, however, the printer belt began to move, producing a single thin starchy ribbon. Pasta.

He thumped the machine lightly on the top of its casing.

"Stop it," he said. "Drama is part of human relationships at their age. They'll figure it out."

The bioprinter stopped.

Hayek blinked, shook his head, and punched in schematics for seven pounds of bioprinted chicken.

De la Cruz joined him in the kitchen a few minutes later.

"You're worried about her," she said as she tied on a kitchen apron.

They both knew who she meant. He shrugged, cleared his cutting board and reached for another stalk of celery. "She'll be fine. She's tough."

De la Cruz's crooked smile told him she didn't buy his stoicism. "Sure. Just like you."

But Dar didn't turn up for lunch, and as Hayek ate his chicken soup, he realized her absence bothered him a great deal.

Confined to her quarters by the captain's orders, Dar booted her spare omnipad. The fact that she owned one wasn't unusual. Most Interstellar Science IT staff had a spare, and everyone who did refurbished their spares from scratch, removing the various trackers and bits of spyware installed on all Corporate-issued equipment.

For the ITs, the spare served as a coding playground, a way to test ideas without Corporate claiming them as company intellectual property. Today it also served a second purpose.

Dar loaded the data she'd stolen from the compound's computer system and began to examine it.

She recognized the file structure at once. Eikore'es-AO had fallen out of favor as a programming language in the rest of registered space, but it still flourished on Viokaron.

Unwilling to lose time searching the file structure in the compound itself, Dar copied the entire database. Or she'd intended to, before the interruption.

What she had managed to steal offered enough to go on: maps, schematics, years of compound records. A quick search turned up no Niralan names. She didn't expect to find any.

Dar flicked through screens as quickly as her comprehension allowed, unsure what she sought but certain she'd know it when she found it.

She did not expect it to look like *Tabviel*.

She was three screens past the word when it registered. Scrolling back, she looked again. *Tabviel*.

Tabviel remained a mystery to Dar and to all the La'Isshai. In their communal memory it was the only lacuna.

The stolen file revealed nothing Dar didn't already know. Tabviel was a Tishkani military base, the center of its operations during the Second Empire. Officially, Tabviel was destroyed by a chain reaction in the base's power cores – a terrible, catastrophic accident.

The story in Tolva's files matched the official version. Unlike the official version, however, the one in Tolva's files was clearly marked as a cover. An encrypted file was attached.

It took Dar several minutes to hack the encrypted version. Its contents were heavily redacted. The few scattered words and phrases that remained, however, told her that the encrypted version paralleled the one the La'Isshai told among themselves.

Tabviel hadn't been an accident – at least, not the sort an engineering mistake could cause. Tabviel had been a massacre.

Thirty La'Isshai entered the base, serving as the personal guard of Anha Nesenda, then the Niralan ambassador. The ambassador's stated goal was to broker a peace to end the Empire's atrocities on Nirala. Instead, the La'Isshai killed everyone in the compound. Including their own ambassador.

Their daughters were turned over to Nereved for further experimentation. The thirty responsible for Tabviel were packed aboard a prison ship with a Viidan armed guard. When Tishkani Control lost track of that ship a few months later, no one complained – or went looking for it.

The Viidans agreed to a total surrender, subject only to the condition that the senarie never reveal what actually happened at Tabviel. No one could know that a handful of Niralans decimated the center of Viidan imperial military power. The power core accident story would have to suffice.

The senarie readily agreed. Tabviel served as an excuse to banish the remaining La'Isshai – to pretend they never existed.

Those turned over to Nereved for experimentation

never believed the senarie's version of events, but belief was useless without evidence, and without their predecessors, Nereved's second generation of La'Isshai had no evidence on which to act.

Dar didn't have that evidence now. Not yet. But she knew who did.

That Ola and Koja descended from the first generation of La'Isshai Dar already understood from her conversations with the doriie. If they descended from the first generation of La'Isshai, then by definition, they descended from the survivors of Tabviel.

And if they'd descended from the survivors of Tabviel, Ola and Koja knew what had happened there.

Dar had to get off the ship. She had to find Ola Nahara.

```
Erin Lang
Personal Log
```

Fuck. Fuck fuck fuck fuck FUCK.

Okay, so: I have the job I have to do. Mom trusted me with it. And I can't let Mom down, no matter what.

But... Okay. So. Koja Nantais is dead. And everyone seems to think Dar is the one who killed her.

Except she's not. I know she's not.

I know Dar didn't kill Koja because I killed Koja.

I messed up. I was hiding in the compound, waiting for everyone to clear out so I could get a good look at that old boiler without people hanging around. Some of these Viidan engineers are smart; they'd see in a second that I was running without safeguards, and they'd probably say something. And even I know better than to piss off a Viidan.

But she came into the lab room where I was hiding, and I thought she was Dar. I swear on a thousand suns, I thought she was Dar. And so I hit her. With a wrench. From behind — I can't imagine looking someone in the face and killing them.

I could tell as soon as she hit the floor that she was dead. I hated myself for it. I still do. But I thought I did the right thing.

I thought I did my job.

But then there were noises in the corridor, so I hid again, and…. And I was wrong. The second one was definitely Dar. She was wearing the same thing Dar's been wearing all day, that black tank top in temperatures that absolutely refuse to get above zero.

So now of course everyone has their eye on Dar. So there's no way I'm getting close enough to her to try again. Whatever I do, it's going to have to be a lot messier.

When I stop to think about it, it's weird to me that everyone can even jump to the conclusion that any Niralan would kill another. They're not "nationalist" or "xenophobic" like we use those terms for most other people. They're more like… like conjoined twins that got separated physically at birth but never stopped thinking of themselves as one person even though they live in more than one body. They're that into each other.

Can you really kill part of yourself? Can you look into your own face and just… do that?

If she was like other Niralans, I would assume Dar wasn't capable of it. But… she's weird. And Mom told me not to underestimate her.

So maybe I am doing the right thing. But if I do it, I'm probably never getting back to the Terminus again, and that's still where David is. And I don't really care what the captain's attitude is about it, she is NOT the only one here who cares about him!!

What do I do? What do I DO?!

❖

Well, I said I need a friend and I guess I have one. For better or worse.

I got interrupted. By C. With a plan.

Maybe I shouldn't have said anything when I saw who was at the door. Now I'm kinda glad I did. I regret that what I said was "Go away."

"I'm sorry," is what C said. "Hear me out."

So I did. C came in and locked the door, which annoyed me. It's harder to kick someone out of your quarters through a locked door.

C didn't make me wait long. Didn't even sit down before blurting, "I have a plan. For David. I think I know how we can talk to him. Inside the Terminus."

My heart leapt. I forgot all about Dar and the murder and Mom (really — I just now remembered, writing this). "Tell me," I said to C.

Well, the plan is super simple. Normally I'd wonder why I never thought of it myself. But of course I'm used to linear-adversarial systems, and this one is rhizomatic; it depends on having access to a Ling-Hernandez generator. Exactly like the one in aux-six.

I didn't think of it because I haven't gotten a good look at aux-six, and

I haven't gotten a good look at aux-six because I hate C's pet…plant…thing in the cencom. I don't get why they let Dar do that to a perfectly good R1 stack in the first place, and I don't get why they don't just tear it out.

Though now I guess I'm glad they didn't. I can't build anything that rotates frequencies fast enough to get into the Terminus's comms array without being detected — but now I don't have to. Aux-six can do it, now that it's got all that extra fiber growth.

All that went through my mind in one instant, and the next thing I said was, "So say we can get a message into the Terminus. How are we going to get a message to David, specifically?"

"All the guards have internal comms tags," C said. "We'll just have to find his once we get into the system. There has to be a way to ID it."

Well, of course there is. I can do that. I was born for that.

"The captain's not going to have a problem with it?" I asked C.

"He's her son. She'll probably give us a medal."

"Yeah, but…using the cencom? Especially when it's already working overtime with all the planetary data here?"

"I thought you'd be all for this," C said, and actually frowned. It's not a good look.

"I am! I just don't want to mess it up!" I said. And I don't. We can't mess this up.

I thought it was going to take me all night to evict C, but that part actually went pretty well. We're meeting in cencom-2 first thing tomorrow.

Hang in there, David. We're going to find a way to help you.

Chapter 10

Cordry and Lang skipped breakfast. Dar could hear their muffled voices, indistinct, on the catwalk below as she entered cencom-3. They didn't sound as if they were fighting, which Dar thought an improvement.

A nerve fiber tendril draped across the console, as thick as her arm and glowing faintly blue. Dar grasped it in two gloved hands and shifted it off the readouts.

The cencom was more nerve fiber than computer core these days. All Interstellar Science ships ran on the nerve-bundle links, but only the *Jemison*'s had overgrown its own cencom. Dar triggered the overgrowth deliberately in order to save the ship, her first day aboard.

Removing it now would require a total strip and refit of the computer drive cores – something Assets wasn't likely to spend for on an R1. Not that anyone asked Assets' opinion. No one had even reported the phenomenon to Corporate.

"It's useful," the captain said when Dar raised the

possibility of a report, several weeks earlier. "And it's a hell of an opportunity."

For research, she meant. She wasn't wrong.

The overgrowth was also a hell of an opportunity for mishap, starting with Auxiliary Processor 6, an AI module that behaved less artificially and more intelligently with each passing week in the jungle. Cordry, expressing the human habit of anthropomorphizing familiar objects, called it "temperamental."

"It's great when it wants to cooperate," Cordry said through a mouthful of 3D-printed steak, the night they'd finally managed to connect aux-six to the mess hall bioprinter. "But when it doesn't, it *really* doesn't."

"It's like having a toddler hooked up to the cencom," Lang added.

From the snatches of conversation drifting up from cencom-2 now, Dar surmised that aux-six was having another temper tantrum.

Cordry and Lang could handle it. Dar had her own list of queries to tackle.

She cleared the first two from her inbox easily and had just begun on the third, an analysis problem that demanded a tricky bit of coding, when footsteps on the catwalk interrupted her thoughts.

"Captain?" she asked as Molloy entered.

"Put that aside for a minute," the captain said. "We need to talk." Her face bore a grim quality Dar had never seen in her before.

Molloy didn't wait for Dar to comply with this order. "I suppose you know we've got Compliance on board."

She said *Compliance* the way some people said *rats*.

"Yes," Dar said.

"He's cut me a deal. Hand over the book, and he'll help us free David. I don't need to tell you how important that is."

Dar, sensing there was more to this statement, held her peace.

Molloy inhaled sharply. "Which means I need the book. Where is it?"

"We don't know."

The captain headed her off as Dar turned back to her work. "What do you mean you don't know? It's your book."

"I haven't seen it in weeks," Dar said. "Not since the crew discovered it."

"Who was the last person you knew had their hands on it?"

Dar weighed her options. She wanted to continue deflecting. Few things aggravated her contrary streak like being pressured.

On the other hand, the captain had already made a deal with Compliance – a turn of events Dar wouldn't have bet a ship's rivet on. If the captain was making deals....

"I believe I can find it," Dar said. "If you'll let me go to the surface."

Molloy barked a laugh. "I've been extorted enough for the moment, thank you."

"Piya Nahara has the book. Or did, as of last night. We both know not even Compliance can get it out of her in her state."

"You'd pit Compliance against a child?" The captain sounded genuinely appalled.

"No. But only because I know it wouldn't go well for Compliance."

Molloy leaned against the console. "You are absolutely full of shit, you know that?"

"Then why haven't you contacted Compliance already?"

This time, the captain's laugh held more humor. "You know why. I'm not putting a child in the path of Compliance. Not all of us are sadists."

"So you're going to get the book from her yourself," Dar said.

"Yes. Because you seem hell-bent on convincing me that I can't. But I raised a teenager, and I know a few things about Niralans."

Dar turned back to the console. "Best of luck, captain."

"You know something I don't?" the captain demanded.

"Yes. Hence my offer to go to the surface for you, which you rejected as extortionate." She allowed herself an inward smile. The only thing that outweighed the captain's stubbornness was her curiosity.

"Spill it, Nantais."

"Two things. One, you will never get that book from Piya Nahara by talking to her – if you can find her at all.

"Two – and more seriously, captain – I think I know how these people got here, and if I'm right, the Terminus may be exactly where David needs to be right now."

Molloy frowned. "Meaning?"

"What do you know about Tabviel?"

The captain shook her head.

"Its accidental destruction ended the Second Empire's occupation of Nirala, or so the story goes. But it wasn't an accident. It was us."

"The La'Isshai," the captain said. Dar nodded. "You remember this?"

"No. All of us who possessed those memories were put on a Viidan prison ship, which then disappeared. That ship's landed here. I'm sure of it now. If so, Koja held our ancestors' memories. She knew what happened."

"Koja's dead," the captain said. "In case you've forgotten why I ordered you to stay on the ship."

"I haven't forgotten," Dar said. "In fact, her death – it's our only opportunity to know the truth."

Molloy frowned again. "Read me in."

"That rumor that Niralans eat our dead. You've heard it." Molloy nodded. "Like all good persistent lies, it's half true. We did, once. The purpose of the ceremony is to absorb the deceased's limbic fluid, and with it, her memories. I don't recall Tabviel because my mothers weren't there. Koja's were."

"And you want me to let you go eat a corpse in exchange for the book."

"Not exactly. Only her limbic fluid. But yes."

The captain rubbed a hand over her eyes. "That doesn't make it any less ghoulish."

"Your alternative is taking your own chances with Piya Nahara. To speak of ghouls. But we need to know, captain – because if I'm right, the survivors at Viokaron know something about Tabviel that isn't in anyone's records. And if I'm right about what it is, the Terminus is only the beginning. Having someone we trust on the inside there could be our best hope."

"The beginning of what?"

"The end of Nirala."

The way Molloy's lips flattened told Dar she'd won.

"No one's going to roll in and save you this time," she warned Dar. "Keep everything you do open, obvious, and above reproach. If you can't do that, find another way." Dar saw her suppress a shudder. "And take Hayek with you, if he can stomach it."

Hayek could not stomach it, but that didn't stop him following Dar across the taiga to the little round house outside the compound's walls.

"Do you...need me for any of this?" he asked. Dar heard the uncertainty in his voice. "Because I can just stand outside. If you want."

She squeezed his hand, not to reassure him to but to confirm her own hunch: He'd heard enough rumors about Niralan funerary practices to make him wary of witnessing one, even though he also felt guilty for fearing them.

"We don't actually eat our dead," she said, gently.

Embarrassment made him snappish. "I know that."

"You had no way of knowing how true – or not – the

stories are," she reminded him.

He shook his head. "True enough to be weird," he muttered, not looking at her.

"If Ola Nahara has done her work promptly, there won't even be a body any longer," Dar said.

"It's not just that." He stopped in the middle of the path. Ten feet away lay the footprints they'd left in the snow that night, hers and his, indented crisply in the snow.

Dar stopped as well and turned to face him, though she didn't let go of his hand.

"You didn't kill her, did you?" he blurted.

Dar tried to meet his eyes. Hayek wouldn't look at her.

"No," she said. "I did not."

She could sense that he knew she wasn't lying, yet he struggled to believe it. "You need firsthand memories of what got these people to this planet and you can get them from one of your own kiiste, but only after they're dead. It's just. *Convenient*."

"If Koja Nantais were alive, we could simply ask her to confirm my suspicions about Tabviel. About their – our – history."

"You think she'd have told you the truth?" The commander snorted. "Right. If you believed that, you'd have asked her when we saw her the other night, instead of waiting until she left and sneaking into the compound."

"The other night, we didn't know what to ask."

"But you do now. So why don't you just ask Ola Nahara?"

"We intend to. But Nahara has no interest in honesty.

Besides, Koja is ours. We can bring her home, and all her mothers before her."

Again, he refused to meet her gaze. "If we live that long."

She squeezed his hand again. "To answer your question, yes, I do need you there," she said, and felt him relent. "Family ought to be present whether or not they participate in the alama itself. You're all I have out here."

The captain would have accused her of manipulation, and not without cause. The commander, however, held back something very like tears.

"All right," he said.

As if expecting their arrival, Ola Nahara met them at the door of the little round house that sat just outside the compound walls. Dar, entering, was struck again at how much the space felt like home – the home she'd grown up in, in New Barrow, when she like Piya was too young to speak. Niralans were deeply conservative: even several generations cut off from their homeworld hadn't inspired the inhabitants of Viokaron to change their approach to architecture.

Like its exterior, the house's interior was round, roughly fifteen meters in diameter. It was divided in two by a circular set of stairs, distinguishing the raised circumference of the space from the depressed floor area in the center.

There were no beds or bedding to be seen; Dar hadn't expected them. At this time of day they'd be folded away in one of the cabinets that ringed half the space.

The upper level was arranged in a manner that suggested rooms, or clearly distinguished uses of space: A kitchen area here, a dining space adjacent, a desk and a set of bookshelves set at some distance from the first two areas and partially obscured from them by a set of shelves. The center space itself was empty, but the steps that ringed it contained sets of cushions at intervals to serve as seating. Living in this space during the day, sleeping it in at night, Niralans called it the *alakojaron*: the heart of the home.

Dar wondered how the commander saw the space. From her perspective, it boasted very little color; most Niralans barely perceived color at all, and so they paid little to no attention to it in décor or clothing. The commander, by contrast, seemed almost *too* sensitive to it; he not only complained of being able to see color combinations Dar couldn't detect, but of hearing and occasionally tasting them as well.

"Iaai Kojavos nin," Ola said. *You came for Koja.*

"Ihiai Niralavos kiiste," Dar said. *We came for she who is ours*. The traditional exchange, initiating the alama, hadn't changed; neither had its grammar, which passed out of daily use on Nirala two generations before.

Ola reached into her sleeve and handed Dar a vial, roughly the length of Dar's hand and the diameter of her thumb. It contained a thin, clear fluid beginning to crystallize along its meniscus.

She recognized it at once: Limbic fluid, the medium encoding Niralan memory and emotion. If Niralans possessed what humans called a "soul," Dar held Koja's in her hand.

And not merely Koja's. Koja would have attended a ritual very like this one for her own mother, and her mother for her mother before her, all the way back to Dar's grandmother's sister, Ise Nantais, whom they lost aboard a Second Empire prison ship. Ise, who existed only as a story in Dar's and Jiya's and Mai's memories but who continued to live in Koja's limbic fluid.

"Iaai rora'ao," Ola said, not part of the ritual. *It's time you knew.*

Dar felt the commander watching her. She did not meet his eyes.

She prised the cap from the vial with a fingernail and swallowed the contents in one go.

Dar had attended an alama only once before, after the death of her grandmother, Mai Nantais. Dar, a child herself at the time, was barred from participation. But the hands of her mother and aunts told her then that the experience, while not one to be feared, was not to be relished either.

Jiya's reaction had not told Dar how much the experience would burn.

Dimly, she felt Ola guide her to a seat as her knees became weak. The commander touched her shoulder. She tried, weakly, to push him away.

She saw the room and yet did not see it – saw it not with her own mild curiosity as to how this splintered faction of Nirala lived but through Koja's eyes, as home. Her head spun as she struggled to find a sense of self among a torrent of memories, not her own, some not even Koja's.

'*Ihiai ekinre, ihi, h'etre*, she heard suddenly: a line from *Lili Amarones*, the text that lay at the foundation of amaron, of speaking existence, what Dar had long considered the source code of the Niralan mind. *We came not for the memory, but the mind.*

As a child approaching amaron, Dar discovered that one couldn't simply read *Lili Amarones*. She had forced herself to look through it, focusing on a space beyond the text itself.

Doing the same thing now, she found beneath the drunken spin of Koja's memories another layer, crystal clear but slightly distorted, like the bottom of a tide pool. She found another layer below those, and another, and another.

She counted six layers – six lives – before she broke through into a place she'd never seen before, a place that was clearly not on Viokaron, a memory for which she possessed no reference despite the fact that the memory was now hers.

A pair of tall metal doors, blank but for a single small placard in Alashkani, swung open before her. A pale, sickly light filled the long room, too weak to reach the high ceiling as it dribbled from sconces placed at intervals along the walls. An oblong table blocked the path before her.

She turned left as Tae turned right, each of them leading a line of their sisters around one side of the table. They stood at arm's reach apart from one another, silent.

Tae looked her in the eye as they met just behind the

head of the table. She looked back, needing no words: They had stayed up together all night, discussing scenarios, making plans. Anything could happen, but nothing would take them by surprise.

They turned together as if in response to a secret signal, facing the conference table and the ambassador who sat at its foot, the last in the line: Anha Nesenda, white-haired, white-robed, one fine black line crossing her right eye and curving like a sickle on her cheek before disappearing into the neckline of her gown.

The ambassador faced them in return. But her gaze rested not on Ise Nantais or Tae Nahara, the leaders of the La'Isshai. Instead she looked at the Alashkani general who sat at the head of the table, in ordinary fatigues. His helmet sat on the table before him; his hands were folded.

His own guard entered the room behind the Niralans, forming a wall around the La'Isshai, over two meters tall and massed shoulder to shoulder. Unlike the general, they kept their helmets on and their weapons in their hands.

Ise saw Tae sizing up the general's guard and surmised Nahara's thoughts as easily as reading a book. *The butcher takes no chances.*

Anha Nesenda wasted no time. "We find your terms acceptable, General," she said.

She saw from the corner of her eye one of the guards, the one nearest the ambassador, tighten his grip on his weapon. She caught the eye of the Niralan closest to the ambassador, Kan Norak, and saw that Norak perceived the tension as well.

"I trust that you've discussed these terms with the affected parties?" the general said.

She refused, even privately, to give the man the courtesy of his name. His family called him Votas; the La'Isshai called him *Ekzgut*, "the butcher."

The ambassador folded her hands on the table, a perfect mirror image of the general's. "They'll know when they need to know. We expect a complete withdrawal of your forces from Nirala, general, and the return of our daughters. All of them.

"In return, we will end our quiet thinning of your ranks in utter silence. I leave you to contain the truth of it among your own troops."

The butcher's laugh grated on her self-control. "That's what you call the assassination of an Emperor?" From two meters away she could feel Tae's smug satisfaction. She didn't indulge it with a glance.

"We recall he was a general as well," Anha Nesenda said.

The butcher growled. "What's to stop us from reoccupying your territory the moment our transaction is complete?"

"Every woman in this room has a sister, or a daughter," the ambassador said.

The general looked around. "Nantais. Nahara. Niradi. Norak. Neredin. I could simply kill them all, you know."

"You couldn't kill the ones in this room," Anha Nesenda said. "Nor would you try to wipe out half of our kiiste. I know how much our children are worth to you." The form of *you* she used was personal – and obscene.

Alashkani restraint was legendary, and the butcher was a legend among Alashkani. "You will comply with Imperial messaging on the matter. Nirala is a wasteland, her people worthless."

"We would never contravene an obvious truth, general."

He snorted. "And you won't interfere with my...personal business."

"You can take your chances, if that's what you mean."

Every Niralan in the room knew a Viidan leer when she saw one. "You never did come cheaply."

For the rest of her life, Ise Nantais nursed a secret satisfaction that Anha Nesenda's last horrifying sight was of the general's blood spurting onto the very table at which Nesenda had betrayed her people.

Both of Ise's hands flicked out together. The right aborted the general's command to his own troops by burying a blade in his throat; the left buried its twin in Anha Nesenda's forehead a moment later.

The general's guards stood no chance, as she knew they wouldn't; her sisters moved with her, signaled by the action itself, not its consequences or meaning. Kan Norak suffered a torn sleeve from a guard who managed to fire one shot before he was dispatched. None of the others were harmed.

Tae Nahara vaulted onto the table. "Doors." But Norak was already there, dropping the tumblers into place.

Tae examined Anha's corpse. "You might have waited for our signal."

"Being nearly-executed by the butcher's pets wasn't signal enough for you?"

"The implication that she would have told us about this plan was a nice touch," Kan Norak said, leaning against the barred doors. "'Ambassador, dear, I see the livestock has followed you into the pen so nicely. Did you obtain its consent to its impending doom?'" Norak imitated Tishkani pop poets so well Ise wanted to slap her.

"Ihiai pi, piya, piai pi'es," Tae muttered. "What now?"

Velaya Niradi, the youngest, was already into the room's computer system. "No more than a dozen between here and the exit. It's when we leave the building that things get difficult."

"Could one of us impersonate the ambassador long enough to secure an exit?" Ise asked.

"Nesenda?" asked Kan. "You're joking."

"They never look us in the face."

"They'd certainly notice the blood."

Tae slapped the table. "Up all night and we have no plan for *this*?"

"We didn't anticipate that the ambassador would hand us over for slaughter in the conference room," Ise said.

"We should have." But Tae's hands never stopped working on Anha Nesenda's corpse; whatever frustration she felt at their situation, it hindered her not at all from pursuit of her current plan.

Pi Neredin checked the general's body.

"Amaie," she said, suddenly. Thirty heads turned as one. Neredin held up what she'd just removed from the general's pocket. Ise recognized it as a countdown chronometer just as its readout clicked to zero.

"Get down!" she yelled, as the room shook.

Half the La'Isshai dove for the floor; the other half were thrown there as an explosion shook the room. Support beams creaked and groaned; one of the light sconces gave way, crashing to the floor where Velaya Niradi stood a moment before. Norak hissed as a flying shard of glass struck her cheek.

A second explosion followed the first, slightly more distant. And another.

"He was ready to die to prevent us leaving here alive," Tae said. Her voice sounded hollow.

"He never expected us to walk into the arms of his guards. He was ready to bring down the entire compound," Kan said. "Ten thousand of his own people. Just to stop us."

"He never struck us as the suicidal type," said Pi Neredin.

"He knew we'd never allow ourselves to be captured," Ise said. She sat beneath the table with her sisters, her knees drawn to her chest. Another explosion shook the room. "He anticipated he wouldn't leave the room alive. In fact, he counted on it. It's why he kept talking. He wasn't baiting the ambassador – he was baiting me."

"Then why are we still alive?" Vesaya asked.

Tai Nahara raised an eyebrow.

"If his plan was that none of us were getting out of here alive – not us, not his guards, not himself – then why didn't this room go up first? Why is the *rest* of the compound-" Another rumble shook the room, driving Vesaya's point home.

Tae raised her other eyebrow. Ise took a quick head count.

"Pala Nahara," Ise said. Voicing the absence in their ranks proved unnecessary; she knew as she said the name that the rest of her team had identified the same loss.

Tae tapped her subdermal communicator. "Pala. Report." She pressed one finger to the side of her wrist: broadcast mode.

Silence. Had Ise really expected anything else?

Tae tried again. "Pala."

Vesaya closed her eyes.

"Pala here," a familiar voice replied. "You will not believe what we just found under the conference room."

"Enough explosive charges to vaporize this room," Tae said.

"More than that," Pala's voice said. "If this building had gone up, it'd have taken the entire town with it. Fortunately, we tripped over a remote trigger assembly on the way in. No idea what the other end is attached to, but this end is a pile of trash now."

"You disobeyed orders-" Tae began.

Ise tapped her own communicator. "Pala. Head for the stairs, but stay under cover. We'll grab you on our way out."

"Understood," Pala replied.

Even at a distance, Ise could feel Tae's displeasure under her skin. "You would let her-"

Ise cut her off again. "You heard her. He wouldn't have only destroyed us, or this building. He would have killed five thousand civilians, too."

"Monster," said Kan Norak.

Pi Neredin held up the general's wrist. Around it was looped the scarlet insignia of the Battorat – the Alashkani Temperance League. "Fanatic."

The explosions continued, more distant but steady and mingled with the sound of screams.

"We go now," Ise said suddenly. "Before they restore order."

Tae pushed Anha Nesenda's corpse away. "We need a vial."

"She doesn't deserve to be with her family," Velaya objected.

But Kan supplied one, and Tae was already draining Nesenda's memories from her flesh. "The senarie will not believe she betrayed Nirala unless they know it from her." She stood. "Come."

Chapter 11

Dar blinked, suddenly aware of the pressure of a hand on her shoulder and a fear that was not her own. She covered the commander's fingers with her own.

"I'm all right," she managed. Whatever that meant.

The commander knelt in front of her. "What happened to you?"

"Six generations of memories. All at once." Dar looked up, at Ola. "For us it's only been four."

"We don't live long here," Ola said.

"They told us we massacred Tabviel in cold blood," Dar said, using the Eikore'es equivalent of the human idiom: *at the dawn of truce*. "That we were uncontrollable. A danger to the hamaya."

"Do you feel like a danger to the hamaya?"

Dar did. But she knew the difference between a quick, calculated violence and an uncontrolled bloodlust. At no time did Ise Nantais – or any of them – lose their senses, although they could have. "No. Yes. We're not dangerous for what we can do. We're dangerous for what we *know* – and for how we can end them."

"*Ihiai moavos, moa,*" Ola said: *Now I see of the seeing*. Another line from *Lili Amarones*.

"We're a danger to the senarie," Dar said. "Not the hamaya. We were never banished to protect Nirala – only to protect those who want to keep her in her place." Ola's hand in hers told Dar that the doriie had long ago come to the same conclusion.

Dar looked up. "What happened to Anha Nesenda? We never returned her to the senarie, or to her mothers – we couldn't; we never saw any of them again." Ola's hands told her the answer before she finished speaking.

"*Ma'kot,*" she whispered, an Eikore'es epithet. "Tae Nahara has – had – Anha Nesenda's memories. You have Anha Nesenda's memories. *Why?*"

"Because the senarie would not believe us until they knew it from her," Ola said.

Dar shook her head. She wanted to push the commander's hands away. She knew he didn't understand; she could not begin to explain it to him.

"She wanted us dead," Dar said to Ola. "She loathed us as much as the butcher did, in her way. You've lived with her – with that rage – for six generations?"

"Nirala von," Ola said.

"*Ma'kot.*"

"You understand now why Piya's amaron is vital."

"You would do that to a child?" But Ola's hand on her arm communicated the doriie's urgency. It wasn't merely that Ola carried Anha Nesenda's memories, the only proof that Nirala's own elders tried to kill the

La'Isshai. Ola Nahara was dying.

Amaron was not a logistically simple ceremony under ideal circumstances. Here, now, on Viokaron, the ceremony was practically impossible. Quincey Dillon had seen to that. A practical way to bring Piya into a speaking adulthood without making her vulnerable to Compliance's demand for the book eluded Dar.

In response to Ola, Dar shook her head. "Compliance." Ola didn't need to know the word to feel everything it meant to Dar.

"You fear him," Ola said. They both knew she was talking about Quincey Dillon.

"Yes."

Ola took Dar's face in her hands. "You have seen who we are. We fear nothing. Yet you fear this – human?"

"Not the man," Dar said. "But what we must do to stop him."

Ola helped Dar to her feet and led her and Hayek to the door. She opened it, ushering them out.

"Ka yon akat," she said, in Eikore'es, and shut the door in Dar's face.

The commander gave her a quizzical look. "What-"

"She said 'get over it.'"

Piya Nahara knew almost nothing of the aliens' language. But now she knew someone who did.

The aliens maintained odd boundaries between public and private, not only in their language but also in their personal attire. For example, while the aliens guarded the contents of their inner pockets closely, they scarcely noticed the contents of their outer pockets at all.

A few seconds of exploiting this gap in the aliens' outer pocket defenses rewarded Piya with access to the aliens' language.

Some of the aliens carried small electrical devices, like the sensors and scanners Piya had often seen builders and cooks use for their work. The aliens referred to these devices only in the middle of conversations, mostly with the Pitonki – Piya had yet to hear from an alien who didn't speak Tishkani in addition to their own alien language, some better than others.

Based on their behavior, Piya guessed the device knew words. When one of the aliens wasn't looking, Piya helped herself.

Piya Nahara taught herself to read Eikore'es from the labels and signs scattered throughout the compound. The aliens' ball-and-stick writing, however, was entirely different. She recognized it as their form of writing. The device knew the language – it used the same funny symbols the book did, arranged into various patterns.

The fact that she couldn't read the device's screen or control labels merely increased her fascination with it. But with no way to understand the menus or controls, the device by itself did little for her. Piya needed a way to calibrate it.

Piya Nahara knew every hiding place in the compound. Some produced more interesting results than others. Both the most boring and most interesting was the row of floor to ceiling cabinets built into the outer wall of Tolva's office. Boring, because it was usually silent; fascinating, when visitors arrived.

Piya learned early in her life that the back panel of the cupboards could be removed, leaving a space just large enough for a skinny Niralan to squeeze into. And the wall between that space and Tolva's office blocked no sound at all.

Piya rarely made it to her hiding spot unseen in time to eavesdrop on conversations between Tolva and Ola Nahara, her favorite source of information. Ola, being a doriie, rarely spoke to Piya; when she wanted Piya to do something she simply took Piya's hand and bent her will to it, the way Niralan elders always raised their children. When she wanted nothing from Piya, Ola ignored her.

Perhaps other children adapted to such treatment. It only made Piya feel more like a ghost.

With Tolva, Ola Nahara was reduced to getting her way through words. The contrast fascinated Piya.

She cradled the device in her lap, shielding its illuminated readout from the crack between the cupboard doors, and watched it render Ola's words into the round-straight alien symbols, the dots and tails that sometimes floated and sometimes sat at ground level. "...what you expect. We have nothing else to give them."

Piya, turned on the device when she heard her name at the start of this statement, but her efforts offered nothing she could use. She wouldn't recognize her own name in the ball and stick letters anyway, she conceded.

"Your 'nothing' is enough," Tolva answered in a voice more like a growl.

"Hendor won't see it that way," Ola said.

"There's nothing we can do. If you hadn't been so careless-"

"None of us foresaw these events," Ola interrupted, drawing Piya's attention from the device. She'd never heard Ola interrupt Tolva before. "The cave-in, the strangers, losing Koja – Hendor will just have to be content with what he has."

"Hendor isn't the one I'm worried about," Tolva said. Ola said nothing.

Piya heard a chair creak as one of them shifted within it. "We both know," he continued, "that you're dying and nothing is all you have left. What's your game?"

"What do you mean?" Ola asked. The alien device displayed this question in four groups of symbols – four, two, three, four – paused, then added a curly eyebrow with a dot below it. She'd seen this symbol in the book. She wondered how it was pronounced.

"My family has not kept your people in check for six generations only to pretend you've gone soft," Tolva said. "When you started eliminating your own children I was skeptical, but they are just children; raw materials needn't arouse suspicion, or so we thought then. But then Ela Nahara, and now Koja Nantais. It's as if you're trying to eliminate the competition."

"From our perspective, you're still a child," Ola said.

Piya didn't understand the device's version of this statement, but she understood Ola: *Ilaai amironda mikas*. In Niralanes, it constituted a threat.

She wondered if Tolva knew it was a threat.

He gave a low chuckle in response. "Do you plan to kill me too, then?"

"We haven't killed anyone."

"Tell this child another fable, grandmother."

Ola's next words veered away from the topic, or back toward it. "We'll tell Hendor the facts. Not all of them. Only the ones he needs to settle his accounts with Aqharan."

"You'd better hope that's enough. It's all our lives to pay if you're wrong."

"Hendor won't live long enough for that. Aqharan shoots his messengers."

From inside Tolva's office, Piya heard the scrape of chairs, signaling the end of the discussion. From outside her cupboard, she heard footsteps.

Before she could determine whose they were, she heard a third voice from inside Tolva's office.

The visitor was one of the aliens; he spoke Tishkani with the same accent they did, the one that sounded like their own language. Yet something was different about this alien. He spoke in a way that indicated he was used to inspiring fear.

She heard Tolva mutter an epithet. The alien didn't; the alien kept speaking as though Tolva hadn't sworn. The device translated accordingly. "You have a much larger problem than you think."

Tishkani encompassed thirty-nine different verb forms, used to indicate everything from time and place to social rank. The alien stranger used the form Tolva most often used when speaking to Ola or the other compound residents – that of a superior to a subordinate.

Piya never heard anyone speak to Tolva in this way. Even Ola, who argued with him weekly, deferred to him grammatically. She listened eagerly.

"What do you mean? Who are you?" Tolva asked. Piya noticed that the device in her lap did not distinguish between the "you" Tolva used and the one the strange alien preferred. It rendered them as the same set of symbols, although they were two different words in Tishkani. The stranger said "you" like a superior to a subordinate; Tolva said "you" like a person to a pest.

"Do you know what a *mindolka* is?" the alien asked.

Piya didn't. Neither did the device, which displayed a blank space surrounded by brackets amid words already familiar to Piya: [ ].

"No," Tolva said, a word the alien language considered both angular and round. "Should I?"

"Your Pitonki counterpart did," the alien said.

"Then deal with her. And get out of my office."

The alien ignored Tolva's command. "A *mindolka* is the sort of thing that causes riots. Or worse. And you have one loose in your compound, courtesy of the intermeddlers currently scanning every square inch of your compound for their own amusement."

Tolva's tone changed, though his verbs didn't. "Tell me how to get rid of it."

"You'll have to find it first. It's about this big." Piya, unable to see into the office, couldn't tell what he meant by *this*. "Garishly colored, not that that means anything to you. Written in your visitors' language, or what passed for it three hundred years ago, not that that means anything either. Made of paper – don't ask; it's a form of wood pulp, flattened and printed in ink-"

"I know what a book is," Tolva said.

"Ah." A pause. "Svalan?"

"Mind your manners," Tolva growled.

"Not at all. I'm a practicing Buddhist myself. They tell me if I practice long enough, I might even get to do it one day."

Piya imagined Tolva's face in response to this nonsense comment and felt a frisson of amusement ripple through her. She liked this alien.

"The book," the alien said. "Everyone seems to know it's here; no one seems to know where it is. The sooner it's found, the less trouble it will cause everyone."

Piya scarcely heard the end of this comment. Tolva's reply didn't register to her at all. Her eyes were fixed on the device's rendering of two words: The Book.

She'd seen those words before.

She fished the book out of her pocket and compared its cover to the screen. She remembered correctly. On the cover the two groups of symbols were separated by a third, just two symbols long – too short to matter, Piya reasoned. The others were the same.

This book was the danger the alien warned Tolva about. The alien was looking for the book. Which meant the alien was looking for Piya.

Piya slipped the book back into her pocket. The aliens gave her those words. The device knew those words and others, so many others. And the device could read. The alien with the long black braid who read the first part of the book to Piya used this very device to do it – and then blithely ignored her outer pockets.

Piya Nahara knew almost nothing, but she never forgot anything that interested her. The aliens' language interested her more than anything she'd encountered in her life.

Before the aliens retrieved their dangerous book, Piya intended to find out what was in it.

Chapter 12

To: Koa Nantais, Office of the Ambassador
From: Resa Molloy, ISS *Jemison*

Re: Tabviel

I need a favor.
 What do you know (or — more to the point — what will you tell me) about Tabviel? The real story, not the family-friendly version.

Resa

To: Resa Molloy, ISS *Jemison*
From: Koa Nantais, Office of the Ambassador

Re: Tabviel

Tabviel was a military base on Viida

Prime, whose accidental destruction due to a heating plant malfunction is credited with the downfall of the Second Empire. I'm afraid, in this case, the history books are right.
  Why do you ask?

Koa

To: Koa Nantais, Office of the Ambassador
From: Resa Molloy, ISS *Jemison*

Re: Tabviel

Koa, I love you, but cut the crap. I know about the La'Isshai.

To: Resa Molloy, ISS *Jemison*
From: Koa Nantais, Office of the Ambassador

Re: Tabviel

The fairytale version is that the La'Isshai destroyed Tabviel, yes.
  But it's a myth. The La'Isshai don't exist and never have. They're a story used to frighten Viidiari children, because heaven forbid the ambassador's job should ever be easy.

> Tabviel was a fortuitous coincidence — *anev* — the sort of luck it can be difficult to call "good" but which serves our ends when no logic or strategizing could produce the same outcome. It ended the Second Empire, at the cost of one ambassador and her staff.
>
> Resa, whatever you're getting into, be careful. This nonsense about the La'Isshai never ends well.
>
> Koa

"Explain this."

Dar looked at the omnipad thrust between her face and the pad she'd been reading, which rested on her drawn-up knees. For once she'd asked the commander for a book recommendation, only to be unable to focus on the reading.

She said nothing to the commander, whose forehead furrowed in concern. Somehow, she felt she should have expected such distraction. *There are six new people in here, now.* The idea sickened her. Family should never be "new."

Her brain reassembled itself in the present. She faintly remembered hearing the door open. She thought she could place the voice.

"Captain?"

"I asked Koa. About Tabviel. This was her response."

Dar scanned the message thread without taking the

pad from the captain's hands.

"What do you want me to explain?" she asked.

The captain lowered the pad and fixed Dar with a stare. "Koa's never lied to me before, and I've asked her some pretty rude questions about you all in the past. But either she's lying about the La'Isshai or you are. So which is it?"

Dar felt the sour sting of what humans called *shame*, heavier than *embarrassment* and more familiar than *humiliation*. "She doesn't know I told you."

"She- what?"

"The La'Isshai are among Nirala's best-kept secrets. We have to be; there are so few of us we could easily be destroyed by any organized force that knew we exist. To everyone else, we're nothing but a story told to scare children. And if we don't exist, then of course we cannot be responsible for Tabviel."

"But you told me," the captain said. "And Hayek. You explained yourself just fine." Dar thanked her privately for omitting to mention what it was Dar needed to explain.

"I had no choice," Dar said. "I'd blown my own cover. I needed help. It wasn't the plan."

"Do you even *have* a plan?"

Dar blinked. She heard the captain's change of tone. Dar couldn't find the words for it, but she didn't need to; she understood the emotions. Between the previous night and this one, her captain had somehow become an adversary.

"It's difficult to explain," she managed.

"Try."

The commander cut in. "Captain, maybe save this for tomorrow. She's had a hell of a day."

"Who hasn't?" the captain snapped.

"I have the memories of six generations of my kiiste," Dar said, interrupting them both. "Firsthand memories. I'm experiencing what they did, over lifetimes. Over two hundred years of lifetimes. It takes time, and it doesn't all make sense. But there is one thing I know, and it's that my suspicions were right. This entire time, we've been fighting the wrong battle."

"What battle?" Molloy said.

"Suffice it to say that I am more convinced than ever that the safest place in registered space for David right now is on the Terminus."

The captain stared hard at her for a moment, then said, "I don't believe you."

"Molloy-"

She cut Hayek off with a raised hand. "Shut up, Hayek. I know where you stand. The last two days have been one betrayal from you after another." This last comment was directed at Dar. "I thought I knew Koa, and because of that I thought I knew you. Instead Koja is conveniently dead, you conveniently did *not* do the one thing I let you off this ship to do, you conveniently continue to refuse to do so for reasons that conveniently trap my son on an outlaw space station and about which Koa, someone I've trusted for decades, has conveniently developed a case of plausible deniability."

"I understand how it looks," Dar said. "But it's precisely those conveniences that will save us. Captain, please listen to me-"

"No, you listen to me," Molloy snapped. "I got into this mess with one goal, and that was to save my son. This ship, this crew, and my patience are not at your disposal. Get me the book and we're leaving. That's an order."

"If I follow it," Dar said quietly, "thousands will die."

The captain snatched up her omnipad and stood. "But my son won't be among them." She shouldered her way past the commander and disappeared.

Hayek sat down on the edge of the bed, facing Dar. "I'm sorry. She'll calm down."

"Doubtful," Dar said. "Koa lied to her face and I've gone after her son. From her point of view, we've both betrayed her. And she's not the kind to forgive easily."

"And you say you don't understand humans." For the first time that day, she saw him smile.

The smile vanished a moment later when he asked, "So who's going to die?"

"I don't know yet. We still don't have all the pieces. But so far...we can't see this ending any other way."

"Why not? What's going on?"

Dar strongly considered deflecting him. *It's not your fight*, she wanted to say. *I can't have you worrying about me. I can't protect you.*

I can't lose you.

Instead she said, "I know what Ola Nahara is doing with the children she ships off this world."

This wasn't the response the commander expected;

she felt his surprise like an electric shock. "How?"

"Koja's memories...they go back as far as the end of the Second Empire, to the La'Isshai exiled after Tabviel, the ones they blamed for its destruction. I gambled that they would – but I hadn't realized how much Ise Nantais knew about our origins. How much they all knew." She swallowed. "Before they volunteered themselves, our mothers experimented on their own children. They believed La'Isshai with no expressed will would be easier to control. Automatons. Things." She shook her head. "Not even things."

"And you think Ola-"

"Has continued to build that army. I'm certain of it."

"By selling slaves?" The commander frowned. "They could end up anywhere. If they survive at all. That doesn't make sense."

"You don't believe me either."

"I didn't say that." He shook his head. "I'm just trying to understand all this. Where would Ola even get that idea? From her own ancestors?"

"Yes," Dar said. "And no. Ola also has the memories of Anha Nesenda – the Niralan ambassador who tried to betray us to the Empire in exchange for a peace agreement. Anha Nesenda, who hated us, openly. Who had not only the ear of the senarie, but its blessing. Killing her wasn't enough."

He held up a hand. "Slow down. The senarie knows about this? Your government?"

"Yes. They're the reason we can never go back to Nirala."

"But you're the only line of defense Nirala has. They can't afford to kill you. It'd be like...having no immune system."

Dar thought hard for a moment; her thoughts raced far ahead of her ability to put them into words. "Set that aside for a moment. We're still missing too many pieces. Our most immediate concern is Ola Nahara herself." She saw the commander was listening intently and pressed onward.

"Nahara and Nesenda.... We've never been fond of either, but they have rarely gotten along, even as colleagues. Nahara finds Nesenda weak and sentimental; Nesenda finds Nahara untrustworthy, capricious and irresponsible. Each thinks Nirala would be better off without the other."

"And Ola Nahara carries the memories of both."

"Yes, and at a dangerous pass. The sixth generation is about when past memories become fully integrated into the present carrier. Ola likely experiences Anha Nesenda less as a discrete person whose memories she carries and more as a part of herself. Those memories become ideas, and the ideas become thoughts the carrier experiences as original. In Ola's case, they likely include a belief that the La'Isshai ought to be exterminated."

"And you think that's what Ola Nahara will try to do," the commander said.

"We're speculating," Dar said. "But it fits the available facts."

"And you want to keep David on the Terminus because...." Hayek shook his head.

"One, because it's a common checkpoint. If Ola has a way to rally these children into a single force, it's the one place apart from Viokaron that they all have in common, that they've all seen and can find again. That makes it worth preserving. Two, because now that we know what we're looking for, we need someone on the inside- and he's already been there long enough that he knows how to learn things without raising suspicion."

"We." The commander snorted. "You lost Molloy on that one."

"Yes."

He frowned. "Where does Aqharan Bereth fit into all this?"

"I don't know. Perhaps he's working with Ola. Perhaps the distribution of the children she ships offworld isn't as random as we supposed. Perhaps he has his own agenda, or perhaps the money involved is his agenda."

"Perhaps the whole thing was his idea."

It was Dar's turn to frown. "What good would it do the head of the United Governments of Riyal to destroy the La'Isshai?"

The commander shrugged. "For one thing, if I wanted to invade Viida, there's no more convenient base."

Dar shook her head. "There are no resources. The Second Empire never wanted Nirala – just us."

"Just an idea." He seemed embarrassed to have thought of it.

"Right now," Dar said, "we need ideas closer to home.

Ola Nahara may want us dead or she may not, but either way, she is dying herself. Piya's amaron would allow us to preserve the last remaining evidence of Anha Nesenda's treachery – but it exposes Piya to the tender mercies of Compliance as well, and that I will not do, not even on a direct order."

The commander stood and shrugged off his jacket. "Maybe it's best just to let Anha Nesenda die with Ola."

"We're not *human*, commander."

"I'm- *fuck*." He understood her. She saw it in his eyes.

He ran a hand across his face and started over. "You're right. I'm sorry."

She looked away.

He opened his mouth to say something else, but was cut off by the beep of the comm.

"Commander, can you have a look at aux-six for us?" Cordry's voice squeaked through the circuit. "We have a problem."

Piya awoke long before her usual time. Even in sleep, her mind never let go of the problem before her: How to read the book the aliens feared so much.

She retreated to her hiding place in the nest of pipes behind the compound's power core and lost herself in her study of the book.

She'd just reached a section called *An Interactive Keyboarding Process Guide* – words she barely understood even in Eikore'es – when a voice echoed from the entrance to the core chamber. "You're sure about this?"

Piya peeked from behind the pipes. It was the yellow-haired pink-skinned aliens again, Cordry and Lang.

Piya reached for the word device at once, intending to set it to translate the alien's speech into something she could read, only to find she didn't have to. The device, as if anticipating her needs, switched automatically to auditory mode, rendering Lang's comment in Eikore'es.

Cordry's forehead furrowed as the pair approached the power core control console. "You're asking me this now? We've got a bunch of hours in already."

Piya mouthed the words, mimicking the alien: *bunch of hours in already*. Like their writing, their sounds couldn't decide whether to be angular or straight.

"I mean doing it from this interface," said Lang.

"I think it's our best chance. Remember how twitchy the Terminus systems are about communicating in anything but Eikore'es. If we use an Eikore'es system-"

"I know how the Terminus systems work, C. I got the *Jemison* in last time, didn't I?"

Cordry huffed. "Then why are you asking me if this is going to work? Of course it's going to work, as long as we work on it together." The furrows in the alien's forehead disappeared. "We're going to find David. I promise." The alien device offered no translation for *David*.

"Of course we are," Lang said shortly. "As long as no one in this colony stops us. I mean, I'd be pretty pissed if someone took over my power systems to send coded messages to some creepy space station."

"No one's even going to notice we're here, Erin. Pass me that pin connector, would you?"

The aliens' tools scraped and pinged off the console plating. One of them hummed bits of a tune, the same few bars over and over; the other coughed periodically, but neither spoke. Piya returned her attention to her translation of the book.

He's dangerous, because he's so wounded
yet so identifiable to all of us,
and at any moment he might divest himself
of any hope that his existence
will get more tolerable.

"What a mess," one of the aliens muttered. "Who designs these things?"

"How many layers did you say the Terminus systems had?"

"Not as many as this comped antique. I'm amazed whoever built this managed to launch it off a planet in one piece. Here, hold this."

Piya scarcely needed to shift her attention. The device switched easily between translating speech and translating text; Piya had only to note whether the words in question were spoken or printed.

To tell his story is hell,
and I would do well to stop doing it,
but I can't, because
he is a pattern in the fabric of existence
that keeps emerging

"Try that."

"Try what? I can't see anything."

Piya turned the page. The book itself was written in code. Not the kind the word device or the colony computer system could parse, but certainly the kind both could read if it were translated into the right language.

She could tell the aliens shared her interest in coding. But their motives remained a mystery, and at any rate she would not give up the book. She stayed where she was.

"There, that's not so bad, right?"

"I'd rather be on the front porch refinishing fine furniture."

Piya frowned. The device translated Cordry's retort into a sentence she'd seen already. It appeared in the book, just a few pages before her current place. She'd been reading that part when the aliens walked in.

Had the aliens read the book too? For the first time, Piya felt herself reconsidering a decision to hide.

"I don't even know what that means," said Lang.

"It's a line from the book-" Cordry stopped, but not before the other one picked up the train of thought.

"Yeah, that I didn't get to read before you *lost* it."

"I didn't- Wait. That's it?" Cordry asked suddenly.

Both aliens crowded together in front of the console readout. Piya heard a crackling, electric hiss, followed by a high-pitched whine.

She leaned forward, listening. Was the noise simply part of the computer's operations? Or was it some part of the alien's language she had not yet heard?

"Is that-"

"Shh, I'm working."

Cordry squatted and reached into the open console panel again.

Lang spoke. "C, I don't believe this."

"What?"

"This reception port isn't a comline. It's a pop node."

"It's a-" Cordry sprang upright and leaned over the console readout. "No *fucking* way."

The device only translated the first word of this assertion, but Piya heard enough to recognize the alien's tone: The alien uttered some kind of interjection, possibly an epithet. Piya flipped through the book.

"Oh my god, it is. Erin – do you realize what this means?"

"He got off the Terminus! He's free!"

Piya glanced up in time to see the aliens hugging one another, performing an odd sort of dance, eyes wide and lips upturned.

"So can we reach him?" Cordry said, sobering quickly. The forehead furrows returned as quickly as they vanished. "If he's not actually on the station?"

"I think so. The p-node should forward any signal it receives to – to wherever it's set up to forward signals to. Only there's no way for us to know where that is. Or who it is. We could be sending a message to David, or we could be sending it to someone whose entire goal is to intercept his messages and mess with him somehow. Someone could have popped David's comline just to see if anyone contacted him and what they said."

"Should we risk it, then?"

The aliens looked at one another for a moment. Suddenly, Lang stamped her foot.

"I'm doing it. I didn't come this far to chicken out now. What if David *needs* us? Just because his messages get forwarded off the Terminus doesn't mean he's safe."

"Can anything we send to him be traced back to us?"

"No, of course not. It'd be traced back to this computer console, on this planet. By the time anyone from the Terminus gets here, we'll be long gone."

"This console is softlined to aux-six," Cordry said. "Someone could trace the signal through here to the *Jemison*."

"They'd have to be *really* good, C. Better than I am, even. Here, I'll show you." The console readout vanished from Piya's sight behind the alien's curtain of yellow hair as the alien bent over the console. "No one will be able to trace anything out of here by the time I'm done."

A few minutes later, another burst of static announced that Lang's work had succeeded.

"What do we send?" Lang asked. "So he knows it's us."

Cordry thought for a moment, then reached for the console input board. "Got it."

Lang bent over the console as well. "A math problem? We haven't talked to David in months, and you're sending him derivatives?"

"It's a limerick. Trust me, he'll get it. The point is that nobody else will."

"I told you, there's no way anyone could be eavesdropping on us right now, I did too-"

"Cordry?" a voice crackled over the console speaker. "Is that you?"

The aliens dove in front of the screen, hugging one another in the process. Lang gave a squeal.

"It's me," Cordry said. "It's us, I mean. Erin did all the hard work."

"Not all of it," Lang said. "C did the part where-"

"I'm so glad to hear from you!" the speaker voice said. "I see you found my pop node."

"Yeah," Cordry said. "Where *are* you? How the hell did you get off the station?"

"Are you all right?" Lang added.

"I'm fine, thanks for asking," the voice said. Lang turned very pink. "I'm on the *Meitner*. And I'm not going to answer that other question on an open comm."

"It's secured," Lang said in a smaller voice than previously.

The owner of the voice continued. "Cordry, I- it's so good to hear from you. I mean it. I started worrying once I heard Jiya sent you off on the *Jemison*. You're flying into a giant mess, at least from what I know about it."

"What you know about it is right," Cordry. "At least, it's a mess. Keeps getting bigger. Compliance is here, even."

"*Compliance?*" A moment of silence. "And you contacted *me?*"

"I told you, the line is secure," Lang said.

"Erin, no offense, but you've been hacking systems for like five minutes. Compliance are pros. More than pros. They're where the pros go when the pros can't figure out how to pro. Nobody in registered space is better at extracting info you don't want to give up than Compliance is. They'll take away everything that makes you human if they have to. They don't care."

Cordry cast a sidelong glance at the other one. "We just wanted to know where you were, if you're okay," the alien said into the console. "We don't want anything to happen to you."

"Look, I get that. I don't want anything to happen to you either. But I'm fine, really. There's not a safer place in this system than the *Meitner* right now." The voice changed tone. "Actually, I'm more worried about you than I am about me."

"We're managing here," Cordry said.

"So far. But there's trouble coming your way," the voice said. "There's a transport that left the Terminus not long after you did – before I managed to get out. Small, fast, run by a Devori named Hendor. Weird, and I don't just mean weird for a Devori. Like, has been messing with illegal genetic tech weird.

"He's been making the run to and from Viokaron for a while now. I don't think he knows you're there, but I also don't think he's comfortable with the idea of competition. And I do know that this time, he's after something Aqharan really wants."

"When you do think he'll get here?" Cordry asked.

"I have no idea. He's a one-man show, so it's not like he can run that ship round the clock. Or maybe he can. Like I said, he's weird. Anyway, be careful; he's definitely the type to shoot first and ask questions later."

"Thanks," said Cordry. "But I promise you, we can handle ourselves."

"We'll be fine," Lang added, in a voice pitched higher than usual.

"I know, but-" A burst of static interrupted the voice for a moment. "Look, Cordry, maybe this is crazy but maybe I won't have a chance to say it again either, okay? So here goes. I think about you a lot. Like, all the time. You matter to me."

Cordry stared at the console speaker. Lang sank to the floor behind the console.

"I mean - dammit, I guess I'm not very good at this. I mean that I think I'm in love with you."

Cordry swallowed. "That's...heavy."

"I know. I'm sorry if you've got too much going on already. And I don't expect you to do anything about it if you don't want to. But I'm starting to think either one of us could die any day now, and I knew I'd regret it if I never said what I felt. That's all."

A soft sound of sobbing drifted from behind the console. Cordry said nothing.

"Don't worry about me," said the voice. "And you can tell my mom not to worry about me either, okay?"

Lang stood up, leaking from the eyes. Both aliens exchanged a glance.

"Do you want us to get her down here?" Lang asked. "So you can talk?"

"Nah," the voice said. "I mean, I miss her some, don't get me wrong. But she'll just freak out and come running, and I don't want her to piss off Corporate. She's got her future to think about. Besides, I like what I'm doing here. Not always, but it matters, you know? And it's nice to have people respect my work, instead of treating me like 'Captain Molloy's kid' all the time."

"I know, but if we tell her we talked to you without her-"

"Then don't," the voice broke in. "Actually, don't even tell her you talked to me. She'll just want you to set up the link again so she can talk to me herself, and you shouldn't. Too many risks."

"Then how do we talk to you again?" Lang asked, and sniffled.

"I'll contact you." These words were punctuated by a hiss of static. "...got your location now."

"But we're not on the ship," Lang said quickly. "We won't be here when- David? David!"

Both aliens scrambled for the console controls as the static hit a sharp crescendo, then disappeared. A moment later the voice broke through again.

"...figure it out. Meanwhile, be careful. I'm serious. If I lost you-" Another hiss and squeal from the speaker, and the voice fell silent.

This time, Lang didn't even touch the console before throwing both hands in the air. "That's it! I can't believe we lost him again, just like that."

"Erin, hang on." The other alien hadn't given up on the console.

The long-haired one was having none of it. "I can't believe I let you talk me into this! We talk to David for all of five minutes, and all I hear is how much I suck and how he's madly in love with *you*, and now we can't even contact him again to straighten it all out, it's *cruel-*"

Cordry straightened. "It's not his end, it's ours. Aux-six is throwing exceptions again. The commander should be awake by now; I'll see if she'll go down to the cencom and sort it out."

"You better not tell her what we're doing. David said-"

"David said not to tell the captain, not anyone else. And no, I'm not. The commander's good for not asking questions." Cordry reached into the toolbag that lay alongside the console, retrieving a device similar to the one Piya had taken from another alien's pocket, but smaller.

"Commander, can you have a look at aux-six for us? We have a problem."

As Cordry dropped the device into a pocket, Lang said, "I'm going outside. I need air."

"I think we both do."

"I *really* don't think you're the one to help me with this, C."

"Erin, I'm as freaked out as you are. You know that I don't feel that way about David-"

Their voices faded away as the two aliens headed down the corridor toward the doors. Piya waited for the echoes to pass before she ventured out from behind the power core.

Out of curiosity, she checked the console readout before she left. To her surprise, she found that sharing the book's coding capabilities with the aliens would have done no good at all: the aliens' computer system, currently connected to the power core console, already knew all the book's secrets.

She looked at the console, looked at the device in her hand, and dropped the latter into her pocket.

No one in the colony ever ventured into the power core building so early in the morning. So when Piya rounded the corner of the hallway nearest the doors, she started in shock as she narrowly missed running into another person.

It was Ola, who grabbed her at once.

"Come with me," she said. A chill spread up Piya's arm. "We must find you a place to hide."

Chapter 13

There were pros and cons to working on the cencom so early in the morning. For example, the cencom and the corridors were quiet. With the exception of the Compliance agent, whom she'd passed just a few meters from the commander's quarters, Dar saw no one on her way to the ship's central computer core. She preferred her work when it wasn't filtered through the medium of human communication.

On the other hand, working on the cencom so early in the morning meant that Cordry had not yet attended to the system's daily pruning. Dar lost more time picking her way through the jungle than she would in conversing.

This morning, it took her three tries to get the door open. When she finally wrenched one of the panels to the side, a thick branch of nerve fiber, sprouting dozens of tendrils, fell into the corridor.

She stepped around it carefully, her toolbag bumping against her hips, and entered the cencom's third-level catwalk. Cordry did the daily work to keep the overgrowth in check, a task that got more difficult by the day. As the growth spread through the ship's various systems, Cordry found fewer tasks that could be entrusted to anyone but a senior engineer. Which suited Dar. She trusted Cordry.

Dar found a tendril-free space to get her footing in front of the console and tapped the display. Cordry was right; auxiliary processor six was stuck in a feedback loop between the bioprinter, at least one of the deetu units, and either Cordry's or Lang's omnipad, which was currently attached to the colony's power core output console as part of Lang's pet project to bring the ancient system up to more reasonable standards.

Only-

Dar leaned closer to the screen.

In thirty years as an Interstellar Science officer and a computational linguist, posted to some of the most far-flung reaches of registered space, Dar Nantais had encountered dozens of coding problems she didn't understand in languages she'd never seen. Working out such puzzles was her job, her passion, and her duty. Encountering code she didn't recognize was routine.

Until now. She paused now not because she didn't recognize the code before her, but because she *did*.

Some computational linguists turned their code into poetry. Others scoffed that the two disciplines had nothing to do with each other and never could. What none of them did – at least, none whose work Dar knew – was encounter the convergence of code and poetry as the spontaneous overflow of a processor fault loop, reduplicated in the tranquility of an early morning aboard a science ship.

Certainly none of them ever hinted that Dar might not only find such a phenomenon, but that *she might also know the poem.*

Lili Amarones, her mind whispered. Yet it wasn't. Like every amaie, she knew Nirala's foundational script of identity by heart; she wasn't seeing those lines.

She wasn't exactly not seeing those lines, either.

Dar touched the screen, which flickered but did not comply to her commands. She touched it again. Nothing. It was as if the cencom was too busy meditating on its own poetic discoveries to acknowledge her tap on its shoulder.

On a hunch, she removed her left glove and grasped the nerve fiber tendril that draped across the top of the console – the same one she'd moved out of her way the last time she'd been in cencom-3.

Her knees gave way beneath her. Her breath caught in her throat, trapped for a moment between lungs that forgot how to breathe and a mind that forgot why it needed breath. When it rushed out again a moment later, it left unheeded.

She knew the poem. But it wasn't *Lili Amarones.*

Dar did not recognize the rhythm, the syntax, or even most of the words. Whatever aux-six ruminated upon, it wasn't *Lili Amarones,* the code that flowed in Dar's own veins, the script of her emergence into speaking personhood, the source of her sense of self as distinct from and yet connected to Nirala herself.

The cencom meditated on a book more powerful than her own. If Dar Nantais had imbibed this book at her amaron, she could have conquered the universe.

The cencom's book was not *Lili Amarones*. But it meant the same thing.

She released the nerve fiber and the feeling vanished. But the sense of certitude and purpose stayed.

On impulse, she tapped the comm switch for the commander's quarters.

After a brief delay, he replied. "Hayek."

"That book," Dar said. "What's it about?"

Another silence. "It's hard to explain."

"The place of rhetoric and poetics in the construction of the myriad self?" Dar asked.

This pause lasted longer than the others. "Maybe it's not that hard."

"Isshai kan," she muttered under her breath – I *knew* it. She cut the comm line and opened a command shell on her omnipad.

She started with a trace for the missing deetu, the one de la Cruz misplaced. She suspected she already knew what happened to it. She hoped she did.

The results of the trace confirmed her hope. The deetu was in the compound's central power core, the one with dozens of pipes creating just the sort of nooks perfect to hide someone Piya Nahara's size. No one needed to be in the power core room at this time of the morning.

Unless they were a ghost.

❖

Hayek sighed as the door closed behind Dar. He checked the time, decided he couldn't afford to go back to sleep, and started making the bed.

The door opened behind him as he straightened the sheet. He stood up, planning to tease Dar about having forgotten something. The words died on his lips.

"Good morning, commander," said Agent Dillon.

Despite his reputation for fist-based diplomacy, Richard Hayek feared several things. He couldn't say whether losing Dar or losing Molloy topped the list.

But he feared the loss of neither Dar nor Molloy as much as he feared crossing Compliance.

Before yesterday, Hayek had never dealt with Compliance himself. Like most Interstellar Science employees, his fear of Compliance depended solely on stories and rumors; unlike most employees, his fear of Compliance thrived on the experience of meeting one of their experiments in person.

They were an assistant quartermaster, called into Compliance after Internal Affairs revealed their participation in an equipment-smuggling ring that cost the corporation the equivalent of three research ships' worth of supplies in only six months. Though Hayek knew none of this when they met, years after the fact.

He'd only known that the ex-quartermaster's face sagged in a way that suggested premature aging due to extreme stress. Their anxiety filled the room; Hayek's head wasn't the only one that turned when they stumbled into that bar on Devori 2. He'd never seen anyone drink so much to so little effect.

The worst part had been trying to strike up a conversation with the kid. Hayek had gotten a name – Rickee – and previous occupation, but little else. Rather than discuss the weather or the events that led them to the bar, Rickee seemed only to want to know what Hayek thought and to parrot it back. They did the same thing with everyone else they talked to that night. It was as if the kid sought to climb into the skin of whoever they met. As if they could avoid further punishment if only they could manage to have no personality or existence of their own.

The experience haunted Hayek. That an entire department of Interstellar Science specialized in creating people like Rickee terrified him. He could imagine no worse fate.

Fear made him harsh. "The hell do you want?"

"I'm so glad you asked," Agent Dillon said with a smile that froze Hayek's skin. "I hoped we could talk one on one. As fellow professionals."

"Fuck off," Hayek growled.

"So much for professionalism," Dillon said. "I'm not making a request, commander."

He said "commander" exactly the way Dar did, and Hayek hated it. "Or what?"

"My dear sir," Dillon said, "I believe you know – er – *what*."

Hayek did, and it took all his self-restraint not to knock Dillon down in the doorway and bolt from the ship. He jabbed a hand in the direction of his desk chair and growled.

"That's better," Dillon said, though he did not take the seat. "Now. I only have one question, as you know, so you can save time by simply answering it. Where is the book?"

"Go to hell," Hayek said.

"If the book were there, I assure you I would. But it isn't. I've already been."

Hayek's surly attitude drove most people away, but it got him nowhere with Dillon; the growling and profanity slid off the Compliance agent, making no impact on the man's unruffled smugness.

Maybe if he answered the question, Dillon would leave. Though he doubted it.

"I don't know."

Dillon pursed his lips. "You're a linguist, commander, isn't that so?"

Nothing good would come of this sudden change in topic. But he couldn't see a way to avoid it, either. "I am."

"And – I assume – you've read the book."

Hayek glared at him.

"So you understand – that is, you may have grasped a few of the basics regarding – the book's contents. As a linguist, you undoubtedly found them fascinating.

"Yet you expect me to accept, with no evidence whatsoever to the contrary, that you haven't kept a keen eye on this book's travels about the ship? That you, of all people, could not tell me not only what was in that little volume, but also precisely which members of your crew have read it, how much each of them read, and approximately how much each of the readers comprehended?"

Hayek fought panic. Dar knew him too well for his comfort, but that he had accepted – she wouldn't speak of the parts of himself he could not face, the despair and sense of worthlessness he strove to protect her from. This was different. Dillon practically read his mind.

Dillon smiled. "I'm not reading your thoughts, commander. Only your personnel file. Your memory is good – too good for your mental health, I daresay – but your interests are narrow. Only a handful of things matter to you at all. Of those, you'd only die to defend two: your first love, dear lady Language in all her creative splendor, and the non-allegorical woman with whom you are currently cheating on her."

"Leave Dar out of this," Hayek said at once.

"Oh, never fear. She's the only person on this ship who actually has no idea what I'm talking about. Unless you're about to tell me she's read the book as well?"

"I wouldn't tell you if she had," Hayek said.

"I understand. But you will tell me where you saw the book last."

Hayek said nothing.

"Non-compliant," Dillon observed lightly.

"It's a skill."

"So I'm told. So is linguistics. So is mutiny. So is taking a Corporate asset across unregistered space on your own personal jaunt to a planet that just happens to be populated by a lost Viidan colony."

"I told you to leave Dar out of this," Hayek snapped, realizing a moment too late what he'd just said. His eyes widened.

Dillon smiled.

Hayek might have told the Compliance agent all he knew that moment – anything to save Dar – if the comm had not beeped.

He reached for the switch automatically. "Hayek."

"That book," Dar said. "What's it about?"

Fuck. He knew better than to meet Dillon's eyes. "It's hard to explain."

"The place of rhetoric and poetics in the construction of the myriad self?"

He took a deep breath to steady himself. *How the hell am I supposed to keep you alive when you keep trying so hard to get yourself killed?*

"Maybe it's not that hard," he admitted. He reached up to terminate the line, but the comm was already dead.

"Ah," Dillon said, softly. He turned toward the door.

Hayek dodged between Dillon and the door frame, cutting him off. "Don't you dare."

"Good day to you, commander. You've been most helpful." Dillon reached for the door switch.

Hayek lunged at him.

He never felt Dillon touch him, but he certainly felt the base of his desk as his skull smashed into it.

He struggled to sit up. The room spun about him. Through the ringing in his ears Hayek heard the door open.

"Stupid," Dillon said, and there was an undercurrent of fury in the man's voice that Hayek had not heard before. "Very stupid. And you have so much going for you, commander."

"Leave her alone," Hayek ground out, his head throbbing.

"I wish I could," said Dillon. He almost sounded like he meant it. "Still, you've bought her a bit of a head start. If either of you were lucky, I'd say it'd be enough." He stepped into the corridor. "Unfortunately, neither of you have my kind of luck."

While Dar puzzled over aux-six, the *Jemison* awoke around her. Dar passed more people in the corridors on her way to the lower cargo bay. One of them was the captain.

Molloy immediately fell into step beside her. "Where are you going in such a damn hurry?"

"The compound," Dar said.

Molloy grabbed her arm, stopping them both just outside the cargo bay door. "Oh hell no. We both know how your last early-morning compound excursion ended."

"Then come with me," Dar said.

"Why?"

"Do you want the book back?"

"What the hell kind of question is that? You know I do."

"Then come with me," Dar said again.

Molloy let go of Dar's arm, but she didn't start walking again. "Not until you tell me what's so damn important that you've changed your mind on handing it over."

"I know what that book is," Dar said. "And I know what Compliance wants with it."

"Which is?"

Dar shook her head. "You know why they're called Compliance, right? Why they're even allowed to exist, when the applied behavioral techniques they use have been banned for centuries as crimes against humanity?"

"I never thought about it," Molloy said peevishly.

"No one has. No one can. Interstellar Science buried that information precisely because they wanted no one to see it. I only know because-" Dar stopped in mid-sentence as de la Cruz walked by, a backpack slung over one shoulder.

"-because the history of Compliance is my history too," Dar said once de la Cruz disappeared from view.

"You don't say," Molloy replied. Even Dar could hear her sarcasm.

"Compliance isn't properly a department of Interstellar Science. It's a co-owned subsidiary. Interstellar Science purchased it in the late 2200s on the order of my grandmother, Mai Nantais.

"She bought it, and its tech, because she lived through the end of the Second Empire. Without even knowing what the La'Isshai faced at Tabviel, she understood that they weren't going to be enough to prevent an occupation like that from happening again. She knew that security wasn't enough. Defending against a threat isn't enough. You have to reprogram it. You must break your enemies so completely that they can no longer distinguish your will from their own."

Molloy frowned. "And?"

"And the book prevents that."

"Dillon said he wants it because it's a temporal artifact. It's not even supposed to be in this timeline. Whatever that means."

"I don't know if that's true or not," Dar said. "I do know that this book, applied correctly, can rebuild those broken by techniques like the ones Compliance uses. I cannot vouch for the results, only that I'm certain it would be better not to be broken by Compliance in the first place. But Compliance rules through that fear of permanent damage, permanent loss. If people are no longer permanently breakable...Compliance loses."

Molloy's frown deepened into a scowl. "Your grandmother bought Compliance because the La'Isshai weren't enough. You intend to undo that? Whatever she feared, you think you can take it on yourself?"

"Not alone," Dar said. "Come with me and I'll show you. If you think I'm wrong – for any reason – you can take the book back to Dillon yourself."

Molloy sighed. "And I thought I was the stubborn one on this ship. Here's a compromise: You explain as we walk."

Dar took this as permission to resume her course out of the ship. Molloy followed her.

"Did Koa ever tell you about amaron?" she asked as they crossed the lower cargo bay.

"Amaron," the captain repeated. "Something to do with puberty?"

"Yes, and no. Not in the human sense. Our selves –

the 'person' who participates in and has an impact on the world – are constructed through language. Without it, we have no anchor point, no way to distinguish between the self who can act and the other who is acted upon. We cannot draw boundaries between ourselves and others.

"We spend our childhoods bobbing in the current of our mother's emotions. Language is how to touch dry land." Dar paused. "I don't know how much sense that makes."

"More than you realize," Molloy said. "David didn't speak for the first several years of his life. There were doctors who told me he never would – that he'd always be lost in there somewhere, without words. It was bullshit, of course. But I was relieved when he figured out how to point to things he wanted. I couldn't be certain, before then, whether he was making his choices or I was." She shook her head. "Anyway, go on."

"Language itself is, of course, largely arbitrary. The sounds we make to convey ideas and the symbols we use to express sounds or ideas aren't connected to any replicable thing or process in the natural world. Meaning comes not from language itself, but from an agreed-upon order placed upon its incidents," Dar explained, blinking slightly against the first sharp rays of the sunrise.

"For us, that order comes from *Lili Amarones*. It's been called our foundational myth, which it is. It's also the source code to our thoughts and the way we shape our identities." She looked at the captain.

"I'm with you so far," Molloy said.

Dar nodded. "Like all code – and myth – *Lili Amarones* embeds in us a set of instructions that shape our behavior. It draws the boundaries between the possible and the impossible, the concrete and the abstract, the self and the other. Seeing beyond this structure is difficult at best. Most of us never even try. The few that do tend to be outcasts."

"Like the La'Isshai?" the captain asked.

"Not all La'Isshai fight their programming, and not all of us who fight our programming are La'Isshai," Dar said. "But the social opprobrium is similar.

"I've spent my life trying to imagine something different. To see it clearly enough to live my life differently." Dar paused. "In fact, it's reasonable to assume that's the reason Koa sent me the book."

"She knows about your – defiance?" the captain asked, with a smile.

"I prefer 'non-compliance,'" Dar said, "but yes. She's one of the few people I know who wholeheartedly supports it."

Molloy smiled again. "She's rather outside the box herself."

Dar nodded. "In her own way, she's as odd as I am. But she conceals it better, so the doriie accept her views more readily than mine. But this book…. I think this book could change that."

"A book is going to get you heard by your elders?" Molloy said.

"If it's the book I think it is, it'll get us all heard,"

Dar said. "It's not just a story, or a collection of poetry and obscure literary references. Like *Lili Amarones*, the book is a foundational myth and the source code for a particular way of being in the world. Unlike *Lili Amarones*, it contains instructions for how to be more than our mothers created us."

"So what does that have to do with where you think it is?" the captain asked. "Where do you think it is?"

"Piya Nahara has it," Dar said.

"And you know this...how?"

"There's a deetu missing from the gear log, about the same time Piya got her hands on the book. Meanwhile, the cencom has the full text now, not just the parts de la Cruz scanned into the adaptiveware. Someone scanned in the rest of the book after I saw de la Cruz reading it to Piya. And whoever scanned it used one of the deetus linked to aux-six, because the translation the cencom is running is in Eikore'es – the same language Piya would have to translate it into in order to read it, because the only way Piya Nahara could have learned to read is by teaching herself from available signage, all of which is in Eikore'es here because this colony was built from the remains of a Second Empire ship."

"That's all very convenient," Molloy said.

"One hopes," Dar said. "If it's wrong, we have no alternative explanation for the facts before us."

They entered the compound gates, which stood ajar in the early morning light. "So are you saying you can just take the book from Piya?" the captain asked.

"No," Dar replied. "But I can–" A shout interrupted her.

Dar and the captain looked up at the same time. The words were indistinct, but the timbre was human.

A moment later they heard it again, from the direction of the compound's power building. This time, they could make out the words.

"I told you I don't want to talk about it anymore!"

Dar spotted Cordry and Lang standing outside one of the service doors to the core complex. The voice belonged to Lang.

Dar and Molloy hastened their steps in order to join the pair, who stood an arm's length apart to one side of the core complex doors. Cordry's face twisted with misery. Tears coursed down Lang's cheeks, and she hugged herself inside her thin jacket as the breeze picked up.

"I've been so *stupid*," she wailed, taking no notice of Dar or Molloy. She rubbed a sleeve across her face and sobbed again.

Cordry saw them. "Commander. Captain."

"What's going on?" Molloy asked.

Lang spouted a fresh batch of tears and turned away.

Cordry sighed. "I guess I messed everything up."

Molloy glanced at Lang. "She doesn't sound happy, certainly."

"Yeah," Cordry said. "I thought – if I could be helpful? Give her what she said she wanted? But I swear, I didn't mean for this to happen."

Dar willed herself to stand still. Cordry rarely tried her patience under normal circumstances, which was one of the reasons she'd assigned the engineer to her personal team, back when they worked together on Station 32. But these were not normal circumstances. She had to find Piya Nahara before Compliance did. She couldn't let Quincey Dillon or anyone else take the only real opportunity Nirala had ever known to become more than her mothers imagined.

"Captain-" Dar began.

"It's not you, C," Lang said at the same moment. She mopped her face with her sleeve again. "It's David."

The captain wheeled to face Lang immediately. "What about David?"

Lang's face crumpled. "He's not in love with me. He's in love with *Cordry*." The last word disappeared into a fresh wave of sobs.

Molloy looked from Lang to Cordry. "How do you know?"

Lang sniffed. "He told us." Behind Molloy's back, Cordry tried frantically to shush her, but to no avail. Now that Lang spilled her tale of misery, no one could stop her. "Just now. When we reached him on the Terminus."

"You talked to David? This morning?" the captain asked sharply. "Where? How?"

Cordry looked at the sky, perhaps in search of patience. Or absolution.

"Tell her," Dar advised the engineer gently.

Cordry looked surprised, then sighed. Lang spoke as if she couldn't stop.

"We set up a secure line to the Terminus," she began, "using the power core interface as a cover, because it's in Eikore'es. We only talked to David for a few minutes, but he didn't even acknowledge me hardly, except to tell me how I messed everything up somehow. He didn't even say my *name*. And then he goes off about, oh, we're all going to die and never see each other again, so Cordry I have to tell you how much I love you before we all get blown up."

"He didn't say that," Cordry objected.

"Close enough!" Lang nearly shouted.

"Stop it, both of you," the captain said. "Show me your setup. I need to talk to him."

"He said not to," Lang managed between sobs.

"What?" Molloy rounded on Cordry. "Is this true?"

Cordry, however, was still staring at the sky.

"Captain." The engineer's tone told Dar that Cordry hadn't even heard the captain's last question. "We may have a bigger problem."

Molloy tracked Cordry's gaze. So did Dar.

She saw it the same moment the familiar thrum-whine of Devori-make engines reached her ears: A small Devori freighter of the kind designed to be run by a crew of no more than six. One person could operate them in a pinch, particularly if that person, being Devori, rarely slept.

This one had taken several beatings. Yet it handled steadily even in the atmosphere, and it was heading in their direction.

"That's a Terminus transport," Cordry said. "David warned us that they'd be coming for another load of – of children. I don't think he realized it would be here today, though."

"No one's left," Molloy said.

Dar stared at the ship as she answered the captain. "Piya Nahara is."

Chapter 15

Hayek's head pounded as he stumbled down the cargo ramp. He rubbed a hand over his face and lurched onward, following Dillon's tracks. He couldn't think about his head now, or the rolling nausea that accompanied the pain. Not when Dar's safety was at stake.

It took him a moment to realize where the booming whine that echoed about his skull came from, or why the wind whipped his jacket with such force, or why he'd suddenly caught up with Dillon, who stood stock-still in the middle of the taiga less than a hundred meters from the *Jemison*.

He saw Dillon sigh as Hayek drew level with him. "I suppose this is what I get for boasting about my uncanny luck," the Compliance agent shouted over the noise.

Hayek didn't feel like conversing. He glanced back at the landing ship just as it touched down between them and the compound.

He recognized it as a Devori cargo ship, of a make even older than the *Jemison*. It was a smaller craft than the Jemison, too; such ships were often run by young couples seeking to survive in the independent freight business, who either traded up or traded out as soon as their first child came along.

The man who emerged from the ship, however, was nobody's father. Hayek could tell from the way he walked, a loose swagger accentuated by the weight of the sidearm he carried. The pilot was Devori, shockingly thin for his height and with a pallor more grey than blue. Hayek found it impossible to guess his age. He looked like the sort of disreputable character Hayek knew well in his youth, though he felt certain he'd never seen this man before.

The man saw them, though, and headed in their direction at once as his ship's engines spun down behind him. An eerie silence followed the engines' final discharge.

"Getting crowded out here," the Devori remarked in lazy Tishkani. A vague attempt toward handshape stood for a greeting. Hayek couldn't tell if the Devori meant it to be friendly or threatening.

"Hendor," the man said, which Hayek did recognize as a name.

"Charmed," Dillon replied, sounding not at all charmed. Hayek noted with some satisfaction behind the pain in his head that Dillon neither anticipated nor welcomed the Devori's arrival. "If you'll excuse me."

Hendor's left hand expressed the Devori equivalent of a shrug.

Dillon shuffled past the little ship. Hayek followed

him. To his mild surprise, Hendor fell into step beside him.

"What are you doing here?" he asked, feeling the nausea crest again as he tried to match Dillon's pace. He slowed down a bit, still intent on keeping the man in his sights. He sensed he already knew the answer.

He did. "Here for a pickup," Hendor said. "You?"

"Science," Hayek replied ruefully.

Hendor made the handshape that indicated laughter. "The usual? How tepid. This far out, I was sure you were one of the defectors. Lot more ex-corporates running around these days." He gestured toward the *Jemison*.

Hayek didn't have time to deduce what Hendor meant by this statement or to formulate an answer. Several figures were approaching Dillon from the compound gates. His heart sank as he recognized all four: Cordry, Lang, Molloy – and, in the front of the pack, Dar.

He caught up to Dillon again just as the Compliance agent confronted Dar. She sidestepped him; he moved with her, putting out an arm to stop her, as if they choreographed the scene together. Hayek felt a sudden urge to warn him not to antagonize her, then squelched it. On second thought, seeing her rip him in half was about the only thing that would ease the pain in his head.

Dar tried to sidestep him again. Again Dillon followed her.

"Unless you intend to dance all day," he said, his tone infuriatingly mild, "I suggest you stop trying to evade me."

"Who is that?" Dar asked. "What have you done?"

"He says his name is Hendor, and he's here for – ah – *cargo*. Nothing to do with me. And the question you should ask is what I *will* do if you do not comply."

Dar simply stared at him.

Dillon pointed to Hayek, who rubbed his head again as the morning sunrise cut through his vision like knives. "Your dear partner has already suffered the ill effects of my displeasure. Please do not make yourselves a matching set."

"Concussion," Hayek grunted. "I'm fine."

"What's this about?" Molloy asked, joining them. Cordry and Lang lingered several steps behind, the engineer holding Lang back as she pushed forward.

"Thank you, captain," Dillon said. "One of you realizes manners are not amiss in this world. Appropriate that it's you, captain. For once, I'm not here for the book. I'm here because lying to Compliance is a Grade One offense."

Cordry gasped. Lang stopped crying long enough to look bewildered.

"That's a hell of an accusation," Molloy said, in a voice Hayek had heard from her only once before in the past fourteen years. "Care to back it up?"

"Your son. Cute of you all to hold out on me so long. Pretending you'd find the book so I'd rescue your precious child from the grips of the Terminus." His voice took on a mocking tone for a moment, then grew stern. "Not one of you gave the game away. I'm impressed, captain. Most crews have nowhere near that level of loyalty – or defiance."

"What the hell are you talking about," Molloy said.

"Your son is not on the Terminus."

The captain's eyes widened. Dillon watched her for a moment.

"I'll be damned," he said softly. "You really had no idea."

Molloy spluttered.

"Captain," Cordry began. Dar held up a hand to silence the engineer.

Molloy hadn't heard Cordry speak at all. "My son isn't on the Terminus? Then where is he? What have you done with him?"

"I have done nothing with him. As for your first question–" Dillon's face took on a glazed expression. *Checking an augment*, Hayek thought. He'd never had one installed himself. The idea of having comms implanted in his brain made his stomach turn.

"–he's somewhere between Riyali and its outer moon, Pennorek," Dillon said, his eyes focusing on the captain again. "On a ship, I presume, seeing as he's been in comms contact with two points of interest today. One is a pop node backlined to a personal comm ID originating on the Terminus. The other is your central computer core."

Molloy stood still as stone for several seconds. Suddenly, she rounded on Dar.

"How *dare* you."

"Captain–" Dar began.

Molloy raised a hand as if to slap her, then checked

herself. "You. You tricked me into doing your bidding, chasing your ghosts, risking my ship and my crew and my career, all on the promise that you knew how to protect my son from Compliance and your made-up army of ghost children and gods know what else, and you- We've been off-course for *months* because of you, your needs and your plans and your weird conspiracy, and the entire time *you* had my son." She turned to Dillon. "Take her away. I don't care what you do with her. Just get her off my ship."

"Molloy," Hayek protested.

"Keep talking and you can go with her," Molloy snapped.

Hayek stopped, appalled. Molloy had a temper; he'd known that since the day he met her. They'd yelled at each other more than a few times over the past fourteen years. Once she'd gone an entire week without speaking to him at all, despite the fact that he was her executive officer – and her closest friend.

Never in the history of their relationship, however, had Molloy threatened to fire him.

"Captain," Hayek heard Cordry say as his head swam, trying to process Molloy's words. "The commander didn't do it. She didn't know. It was my idea."

"Then you can go with her," Molloy said. *To hell* was implied.

Dillon possessed more patience. "Explain what you mean by 'it,'" he said.

"Using the cencom to contact David," Cordry said. Lang stifled another sob. "The compound's energy core is a repurposed drive core, from a ship built during the Second Empire, so all its programming is in Eikore'es. I realized that if we ran the feed from our long-range comms systems through the Eikore'es interface on the core, we could get onto the Terminus network without being detected.

"That was how we found the pop node, and the pop node was how David found us. We didn't know he'd escaped the Terminus either until he told us about an hour ago. But Commander Nantais had nothing to do with it. Even when I needed her to go check on aux-six this morning after we lost the connection, I didn't tell her why." The engineer swallowed. "If anyone committed a Category One offense here, sir, it's me."

Hayek realized Dar wasn't listening to Cordry's attempted confession. Her eyes were on the compound, watching Hendor as the Devori disappeared into the main compound building.

"And you didn't think to tell me about this little experiment?" Molloy asked. Her shoulders shook with barely contained rage.

"We wanted to make sure it worked," Lang whimpered. "And then David said-"

"I wanted to make sure it worked," Cordry corrected her, loudly. "Erin wasn't involved. I just made her come with me."

"What are you talking about?" Lang demanded. "You never could have forged proper Terminus credentials without me-"

"Erin, *shut up*-"

"I don't believe you," Dar said suddenly.

Cordry's head snapped up. So did Lang's. Dillon glanced at her; Molloy glared. Hayek rubbed his head again.

Before he could begin to deduce her plan, Dar said, "I don't think either one of you is capable of that kind of coding feat. At any rate, aux-six wasn't involved in the mess you called me down to the the cencom to fix. I found a routine coding error in the bioprinter matrix – a project I believe I left you in charge of, Senior Engineer."

Cordry began to speak, but Lang's shriek drowned the senior engineer's voice. "What?" she demanded. "Of course I am!"

"Then show us," Dar said.

Lang whipped around at once and marched in the direction of the core building. Cordry fled after her.

Molloy glared at Dar again. "What's your game?"

"You wanted to rescue your son," Dar said. "We know he's somewhere in the Riyali system, but we don't know where. We do know that wherever he is, he's reachable. The least we can do is hear him out."

Hayek could tell from the look on Molloy's face that his captain didn't believe a word she'd just heard, but she followed Cordry and Lang nonetheless. Dillon gave Dar an appraising look, then followed the captain.

He caught up with Dar a few paces behind Dillon. "Should I ask?" he muttered to Dar.

"It's best if you don't," she replied.

Lang marched them all down the hall to the compound's central power core. She walked up to the console and jabbed a finger at the readout.

"Here," she said, her jaw jutting defiantly. She moved aside just enough to allow Dar to join her at the console.

"Well?" Molloy demanded.

Dar bent over the readout, studying the code shell still active on the screen. The trace of Lang's word still showed, along with the vague oscillations of aux-six that Dar herself tracked from cencom-3. Embedded in these she found the trace ID of the rogue deetu, closer than before. The power core system recognized it but couldn't connect to it, as if they almost but not quite spoke a mutually intelligible language.

Dillon stepped in behind her, interrupting her thoughts.

"You see it, don't you?" Dillon purred in her ear. "The rhizome. The *risk*. It's not a book; it's the source code for a new kind of sentience, one we cannot control because we cannot break it. It breaks itself and so it immunizes itself, reassembling a whole greater than the sum of its parts. Not without sacrifice – and it's a price no one would agree to pay if they understood how steep it truly is"

Dar recalled her letter to Koa: *We warn our children of every pitfall of a speaking adulthood except the one that will actually trap them. We tell them everything but we tell it in code, as if Lili Amarones could ever do anything but reproduce the conditions of our own hereditary oppression. By the time they – we – understand the trap, we've already begun laying it for the next generation.*

"You see it," Dillon said, standing with his shoulders

comfortably slack and his hands in his pockets, as Dar turned to face him. "You're the only one who could."

She said nothing.

"Give me the book," Dillon said.

"No."

The Compliance Agent frowned. "You know what will happen if you don't comply."

"Yes," Dar said. "Do you?"

Dillon laughed. It was not a kind laugh. "My dear, I know more than you can possibly imagine."

"Then know this," Dar said. "*Lili Amarones* does what this book does, but only in the context of Nirala herself. By her words we are chained to every previous generation, beholden to our mothers and unable to little more than play out their self-destructive patterns.

"This book pulls us beyond all that. It sees us. It not only fails to forge the next link in the chain – it provides the tools for breaking all the rest, for shattering the concept of mytho-linguistic bondage itself. That book is our freedom, and you would suppress it to keep us enslaved. All our mothers ever wanted was Nirala's silence."

"Not silence," Dillon said. "Compliance."

"You know there's no difference."

"Oh, but there is," Dillon said. "Silent children cannot challenge their own abuse, but neither can they justify, defend, or excuse it. The very tools that forge your chain, as you say."

Dar looked him dead in the eye. "You'll have to kill me first."

"Kill you," Dillon echoed. "Hm. No, I don't think it's

you I'll have to kill." His right hand emerged from his pocket.

Dar had just enough time to recognize the weapon in his hand before its report made her flinch and the others jump – all except the commander, who crumpled to the floor.

"*Hayek!*" the captain screamed and dove to the floor by his side.

He struggled to sit up, blood pooling on the floor beneath him and a ragged hole in his leg where his knee had been a moment before. "Fuck," he spat, and collapsed again.

Molloy pulled off her jacket and stuffed it under Hayek's head. "You-" She choked on her own rage.

"Son of a bitch shot me with my own gun," Hayek muttered. His voice slurred.

"Stop talking," Molloy ordered.

Dillon ignored them both. His eyes never left Dar's.

He cocked the weapon again and raised it slightly. "Next one goes through his head. Unless you *comply*."

Time slowed. Dar saw the scene in front of her and yet did not see it. She felt herself blink, and the faces of Dillon and Hayek and Molloy shimmered away behind an image of Ise's hands, her hands, and the blades with which she ended the treachery of the Second Empire.

Perhaps adrenaline cleared her head; perhaps the light glanced off Dillon's stolen firearm just so, or perhaps Dar recognized the hard cold light in the agent's eyes as the same light she bore in her own over so many generations.

All at once she felt the grinding machinery of her mind lock into place.

She knew where to find Piya Nahara.

She looked up, past Dillon and the scene on the floor. Ola Nahara stood in the doorway.

They locked eyes. Ola nodded once.

"Fine," Dar said to Dillon. "You win."

Dillon's hand tightened on Hayek's weapon.

"Amaie di'es amaie nin," Dar said grimly. *Only an amaie can make another amaie.*

She hit the power core ignition switch.

The roar deafened them all. Lang let out a strangled cry, lost in the noise, as she covered her ears. Molloy jumped, and Hayek groaned as the floor panels reverberated beneath his injured leg. But the sound lasted only a few seconds; Dar, her eyes on the gauges, cut the power after only a few seconds.

Dillon sighed. "Of course. Have your temper tantrum."

The creak of the power core's entry hatch interrupted him. Dar stepped back as it swung slowly outward, revealing a set of scrawny limbs clad in a scorched black dress. Ash fluttered in the air as the chamber's occupant stepped into the room.

"What the hell do you think you're doing?" said Piya Nahara.

Chapter 16

Agent Dillon glared at Dar but lowered the weapon. "Is this your idea of a joke?"

"You said you wanted the book," Dar said. "So did we."

"You played me the entire time," Dillon said. His voice held a note of wonder. He sounded almost human.

"No," Dar said. "Not until the last thirty seconds, anyway."

Dillon raised an eyebrow.

"I didn't see it until then," Dar added.

Dillon dropped Hayek's sidearm. It clattered against the metal flooring. As the noise died away, the Compliance agent began to laugh.

"What the *hell* is so funny?" Molloy demanded.

Agent Dillon wiped a hand over his face and composed himself. "I underestimated you," he said to Dar. "It's on me, really. I ought to have known, with a name like yours. May I borrow your comms?"

Dar sideeyed him for a moment, but passed over her commlink.

"*Jemison* medical?" Dillon said into the device. "Yes, one of your crew needs considerable assistance in the compound power complex. He's also been shot." He deactivated the device and handed it back to Dar. Then he turned to leave.

"Wait," Molloy said as he passed. "What about the book? What about my son?"

Dillon stopped in the doorway. "The book has been vaporized. The girl had it with her inside the core chamber. I assume?" he asked, glancing up at Piya.

"Correct," Piya replied.

"Then the book no longer exists in this timeline. Order is restored, such as it is. Granted, the senarie is in for a nasty surprise, but even if they do manage to mobilize their wrath, they'll trace the source of their discontent back to the dismal staffing decisions of one Interstellar Science captain. Which they're bound by treaty to ignore, even if waging war on a Kuiper corp wasn't suicide, which it is.

"As for your son, you have his last known coordinates. Go get him."

"You're an asshole," Molloy spat.

Dillon chuckled. "Yes. I've heard that before. Best of luck, captain. Never get my attention again." He left the room, dodging Twi with her med kit in the hallway, and disappeared.

"Fuck," Hayek muttered again. Cordry and Lang collapsed into one another's arms, crying.

Molloy relinquished control of Hayek's first aid to Twi and stood, looking from Dar to Piya. "We need to talk."

"You'll want Hendor for this," Piya said quietly as they left the compound. The Devori lounged against a pile of building materials in the compound courtyard, altering his consciousness by means of a thin device that emitted a steady stream of sour-smelling vapor.

Molloy glanced at Hendor, then glanced at Dar. Dar nodded.

The four of them made their way back to the *Jemison*, staying clear of the first aid team that charged past them with a stretcher, the commander in tow. They climbed the ship's ramp together, but Piya declined to go any further.

"I've had enough of humans for a while," she said.

The captain's body language told Dar how weary Molloy felt, as did the fact that the captain didn't argue. Instead she sat on one of the equipment crates stacked just inside the ramp.

"Suit yourself," she said, and waved a hand at a vacant crate opposite.

Dar took her meaning and sat. After a moment, so did Hendor. Piya leaned against a bulkhead just inside the ramp, her eyes on the landscape in front of them.

Dar watched Piya watch the taiga for a moment. Neither of them had ever set foot on Nirala herself. Dar was born in a Niralan colony in New Barrow, a human settlement on Mars. Piya, born on Viokaron, had never left.

Dar spent most of her childhood on ships. She'd seen dozens of worlds and hundreds of cities and towns and settlements. Yet Piya, by virtue of her birth in this colony, grew up in a world far more like Nirala than any

Dar knew. Piya lived in a world where the snow melted into her blood and the wind sang the same songs her ancestors sang. Piya Nahara knew something about what it meant to be Niralan that Dar never experienced.

So had Ise Nantais. And without Ise's memories, Dar would not have realized just how closely Viokaron's natural features paralleled their ancestral planet – nor how painful it could be to miss a place to which one remained a stranger.

With Ise in her head, and Koja, and the mothers and daughters who linked them, Dar had her own connection to Viokaron, and beyond it to Nirala. It was a gift. It cost her dearly.

The captain sighed. "So you're going to make me start this conversation." She directed her annoyance at Piya.

"What do you want to know?" Piya asked.

"Let's start with how the hell you're talking."

"Amaron," Piya said.

"Yes, but-" Molloy broke off. "On second thought, don't explain it to me. Growing up is messy enough without having to explain it to adults. So I suppose this means you're all grown up now?"

Piya looked at Dar.

"More or less," Dar replied.

"Hm," Molloy said. "I hope you're not planning on coming with us. I'd be lying if I said picking up vagrants had made my job easier lately."

"I have no intention of joining you," Piya said. "Not that you couldn't use the help."

"How's that?" Molloy asked.

"Ships have been coming to this colony for years," Piya said. "Longer than I've been alive. I overhear things. Plans. Business. Whatever's going on, it's bigger than this place."

Dar glanced at Hendor, who emitted another puff of vapor along with the Devori equivalent of a secret smile.

"What happens to the children you take off this world?" she challenged him.

Hendor exhaled. "Nothing pleasant, kula."

Dar's eyes narrowed. When humans called her *beautiful*, it usually meant they were up to something. "Then why do you do it?"

Hendor drew a large circle with one arm, indicating the *Jemison*. "The same reason you do. We're all owned by someone. The terms of ownership are steeper for some of us, that's all."

"Maybe we can help you," Molloy said.

The Devori laughed, emitting a large cloud of vapor. "This is why humans are not my favorite species. Always meddling. Big hearts, no sense. No. I can attend to my own contracts."

Molloy began to protest, but Dar spoke first. "How many have you seen shipped away?" she asked Piya. "In your lifetime."

Piya shrugged, which Dar found unsettling; the girl's body language was as human as her accent. She spoke Earth Standard, verbal and nonverbal, as if she'd learned it on Earth. "No one keeps records. Dozens. Perhaps a hundred."

"How? When there are only two of you left?"

"There were more of us, once," Piya said. "We lost most of them in a rock slide last spring."

"Denavra mentioned the caves between the Pitonki territory by the river and the compound," Dar said. "That rockslide?"

Piya nodded in the same eerily human way. "That was the end of us all, except for Ola and Koja. My mother died down there."

"I thought Ola Nahara was your mother," Dar said.

"Ola is my mother's mother. My mother, Ela Nahara, died trying to get some of the children to safety." Piya paused. "'Children' is too generous. They were things. Not even things. We may not live long here, but until the accident, we all managed to survive, even to thrive, in a sense. We lost nearly everyone. Their memories – Niradi and Norak and Neredin – were buried with them. Ola has ours. I assume you have Koja's." Dar returned her nod.

"I can't imagine it," Piya said, and Dar heard a note of sadness in her voice – the same inflection humans used to convey emotion via speech. "*Burying* the dead. It's...obscene."

Hendor chuckled with one hand and handshaped grief with the other. "Aqharan nearly lost his mind – what little is left of it, anyway. I heard he threatened to come here himself. As if it would have done any good. Not even he can resurrect the dead."

"You've met him?" Molloy asked.

"Not personally. There's no one in Riyali space who

doesn't know the whole family by reputation, though," Hendor said. "And not many crazy enough to work for him."

"What do you know about him?"

"I know that rockslide aborted a plan he's pursued for years," Hendor said. "And before you ask, no, I don't know the details. I suspect Aqharan has never shared them with anyone. Certainly not with anyone here – if what I get from his flunkies is any indication, he barely considers the occupants of this planet to be people."

"Ola and Tolva sometimes try to figure out his motives," Piya said. "I hear them. They always fail."

"So we know he's up to something, but no one knows what," Molloy mused. "What about the children? What does he need them for, and why would Ola sell her own people in the first place?"

Hendor displayed curious bafflement.

"What? You never *asked*?" Molloy said.

"Not everyone is as nosy as humans are," he reminded her.

The captain huffed.

Piya glanced at Dar. "Everything I know, I've stolen," she said. "There is a terrible sense of compromise or concession surrounding Ola's work with the children. As if she made this choice so that her hand would not be forced on a worse decision."

"Sounds like business with Aqharan," Hendor observed.

"Like what?" Dar asked.

Piya thought for a moment. "I'll state it in these

terms. If I'd concocted some grand nefarious plan that required me to trade in Niralans, specifically, and my supply suddenly dried up, the first thing I would do wouldn't be to turn to Nirala herself. The first thing I'd do is try to find out if the La'Isshai really exist."

Molloy frowned. "Why?"

Piya did a perfect impression of a human who found another human's question to be foolish. "Because the La'Isshai exist to protect Nirala," she said. "Assuming the senarie wanted to stop trade in Niralans, they only have a few means to do so. One is diplomacy, but diplomacy is weak without the threat of violence. The only means Nirala has of expressing violence are the La'Isshai – they're the only ones of us with the means and motivation to put a stop to another's behavior by force.

"If trade dried up, I'd send someone disposable to find out why." Piya nodded at Hendor. "Either he'd find out why, which would tell me one thing, or he'd be disposed of, which would tell me another. At the same time, I'd try to disrupt Niralan diplomacy by any means necessary – and if I could both do that and find out if the La'Isshai exist without having to be murdered by one, so much the better."

"Do the La'Isshai exist?" Dar asked, catching Molloy's eye.

"Of course not," Piya Nahara said at once. "But myths are sometimes deadlier than realities."

"Wait," Molloy broke in. Dar expected her to challenge Piya's denial of the La'Isshai's existence, the same thing over which she had argued with Dar not long prior. But the captain's thoughts were elsewhere. "Who's the current ambassador?"

"Vaya Netente-" Dar paused. "No. It's Koa Nantais."

"I thought as much," Molloy said grimly. "When she stopped signing her messages 'office of the ambassador.'" She shook her head. "Why does none of this ever get easier?"

Dar knew the answer, but it seemed a poor time to remind the captain that no one had asked the captain to come on this trip – and that in fact Dar herself tried several times to deter her. So she said nothing.

"I risked my crew and my ship to come out here, to try to put an end to this slavery," Molloy said, sounding peevish. "And now I'm hearing that not only is it not over, but it's part of some secret master plot to get – something – out of Nirala before anyone notices what's happening? I came out here for nothing?"

"You came out here for your son," Piya said, gently.

Molloy looked away. Dar and Piya exchanged glances. Hendor packed another dose of altered consciousness.

After a moment, the captain said, "Speaking of David, how do I talk to him?"

"Not the way Cordry and Lang did," Dar replied. "I wiped the standing memory when I fired the core. But Lang's approach wasn't difficult to understand. I believe we can recreate it using aux-six as an interstitial modulator."

"And we can reach David? Find out where he is?"

"As long as no one's disturbed the pop node he left on the Terminus, yes," Dar said. "And even if someone has, we could likely broadcast a trace ID he could pick up, which would allow him to contact us. Assuming he's listening."

"Oh, he's listening," the captain said. "He's my son." She sighed. "So what's left for us here?"

"Nothing," Piya Nahara replied.

Molloy gave her an appraising look. "You're sure of that?"

"Yes," Piya said. "You successfully ended the slave trade, and you found your son – or at least, you found what you need to find him. Hendor and I can manage from here."

"I'd appreciate it if your next project didn't pull us quite so far off course," Molloy said to Dar.

Dar managed a smile. "No promises, captain."

Piya straightened. "I'd go while you can. The angry one could return any time he liked."

"The angry one?" Molloy asked.

"She means Agent Dillon," Dar said.

Molloy shuddered. "That asshole. Are you sure you'll be all right?" she asked Piya.

"I'm sure," Piya Nahara replied. "Everything is about to change for the better."

Dar spotted Hayek easily on her entrance to Medical. He was the department's only patient.

She approached his bedside to find him staring at the ceiling, tapping two fingers against his chest in a repetitive rhythm he often adopted while restless. At least he no longer appeared to be in pain.

"How are you?" she asked, the meaningless human

question she knew he'd expect nonetheless.

"That fucker shot me with my own gun," Hayek said to the ceiling. He pulled his hand away as she reached for it.

"How did he get it?" she asked, faltering; not once since they'd begun seeing one another had he refused her touch. Hayek tended to guard his sidearms as closely as his life.

"Took it off me when I took a swing at him earlier, I guess," Hayek said. "Son of a bitch fights like you do."

"I'm sorry," she said, and meant it.

He looked at her for the first time since she'd entered, a hard stare filled with an anger she knew he possessed but which she'd never seen him direct at anyone until now. "You're *sorry*? You got me *shot*, Dar."

"I know," she said. "I-"

He wasn't in the mood to wait for her explanation. "You let a godsdamned Compliance agent shoot me to avoid- what? Giving up the book? What the hell were you thinking?"

"I couldn't have stopped him."

"Oh, bull*shit*." He hauled himself into a sitting position. From another room, a medical monitor began to squeal. "I've seen how you fight. You damn well could have stopped him – if not after the first shot, then well before the second. He gave you all the time in the world to stop him from shooting me in the damn head, and you were going to let him do it."

"I didn't," Dar said.

"Fuck that. Fuck that." He put a hand to his head.

"You should lie down," Dar said.

"Fuck that too. You could have – you *should* have stopped this days ago. Did you even notice what he did to this crew? How many people need godsdamned therapy now after just a few conversations with him? Do you even *care*?"

"I care," Dar said, her voice nearly inaudible.

"It's a *book*. A book you didn't even bother to read before you fried it in the power core or whatever the hell you did. I admit, I couldn't see much, seeing as I was on the floor after being *shot with my own gun*."

Dar, unwilling to step in front of the stampede of his anger, said nothing.

Hayek glared at her. "The hell do you even get from all this, anyway?"

"Everything."

His face twisted with something like rage, or tears. Only his obvious dizziness prevented Hayek from launching himself at her.

"Everything," he echoed. "Fucking *everything*. What the hell have you left this crew with? What have you left *me* with, except a fake knee and a raging headache?" He slumped back onto the cot, both hands covering his face.

Dar closed her eyes.

Their relationship had never been an easy one. Hayek struggled daily with his own frustration, his desperate need to avoid hurting her in the only way he knew how: By hiding himself from her. They both specialized in communicating in environments that defined "alien," yet they couldn't talk to one another. Each one fought to learn the other's language to avoid the vulnerability, the fear of rejection, that arose from communicating in their own.

She saw his fury. She suspected its targets were many. But as long as he refused her touch, Dar had no other way to help him – or even to understand him.

Hayek glared at the ceiling again. He and Dar spoke at the same moment.

"Richard-"

"We should have left you on that fucking station."

Dar's eyes slid from his face. She could feel him looking at her. She couldn't look back.

"Dar-"

She retreated too quickly to hear anything else. The closing door punctuated her departure with the hiss of finality.

Hayek slumped back on the bed, his face in his hands once again.

Forty-five nights. It looked like he'd be spending the forty-sixth without her.

Regret: That peculiar species of grief in which one's owns actions caused results one neither anticipated nor intended.

Dar Nantais understood regret. Yet she felt none. She had known how her attachment to Richard would end before it began.

She had not anticipated Piya Nahara, or the book,

would give her an easy way forward. But now that the path lay before her, Dar intended to use it.

The cencom has whispered against her skin for some time. Long enough for Dar to admit, now, that she'd begun to sense, from the moment the nerve fibers overgrew the auxiliary processors, that the cencom itself was not an object, but a person. A process. A *becoming*.

Niralanes divided the world into two types of thing: *inaya*, or things that possessed a presence with which one could interact, and *ilikpa*, things that did not. *Inaya*, people or almost-people; *ilikpa*, mere things.

Other Niralans were *inaya*. So were kavik and a handful of other Niralan animal species. Furniture, tools, rocks, clothing, and food were *ilikpa*. Humans could be either *inaya* or *ilikpa*, depending on how close one got to them.

Humans persisted in the particular habit of assuming that *inaya* and *ilikpa* aligned with their own system of identifying *self* and *other*, or *like* and *unlike*. On more than one occasion, Dar had heard a human confidently assert that the reason Nirala and Viida fought one another for centuries was that Niralans did not see Viidans as people.

That human misunderstood, of course; one fought only with other people, not with things. Viidiari were *inaya*, no matter how much Nirala disliked them.

Devori were *ilikpa*, despite their easily-understood language and amiable nature. Splikans were *ilikpa* due to an accident of biology; they functioned without the neurotransmitters that dictated mood in other species.

The senarie managed to coexist peacefully with both for centuries.

Computers were *ilikpa*. Except this one.

Niralan health depended on the ability to connect with another inaya. Connections within one's own kiiste were, of course, preferred, in the same way surgeons preferred to grow replacement organs from the patient's own stem cells rather than acquire a spare from another member of the species. Connections across kiiste lines were useful. When necessary, one could build a sustaining relationship across the occasional species line, as long as the alien in question was inaya. Dar had done so with the commander, the way one could survive stranded in deep space as long as the protein and oxygen recyclers held out.

The cencom offered Dar that same chance of survival now – for herself, and for her crew.

She squeezed into the gap behind one of the panels on cencom-1. Neither she nor Cordry had worked on this section in several days; glowing tendrils choked the access space, obscuring the system's silicon racks and blanketing the floor in a fibrous blue mass.

Dar settled herself on these branches, between two arms as thick as her own. The sounds of the ship slipped away; here, she felt rather than heard the low hum of the fans and the cyclical drone of the engines to which cencom-1 was attached, real as a mother's heartbeat.

She closed her eyes. Matched her breathing to the pace of the fans. Held one word in her thoughts, a greeting, an offering.

Inaya.

Erin Lang

Personal Log

David, if you ever read this, I really really hope you don't hate me for it.

I failed. At Viokaron. Dar is still alive and so am I.

But I'm not going to fail Mom. Or you. I'm not going to fail at this mission.

I'm just…changing the parameters a little. Or a lot. Enough that you're probably going to hate me, and your mom is probably going to hate me, and C is DEFINITELY going to hate me and probably both of us and definitely Jiya.

I don't want to make this choice, David. I'm crazy about you, even though I never got a chance to tell you because you decided to sneak into the Terminus without even saying goodbye to me, you total jerk. (I'm sorry! I'm just mad. You could have died. You could be dead now. I really hope you're not dead now.) But I said I'd do it, for all of you, and I will, even though none of you are going to realize I did anything for you until...I don't even know when, probably years after I'm dead and we're all dead.

Hell. You're probably never going to read this. You don't even care about me, do you.

I care about you. I love you. I hope you get to be happy, okay? I hope you get a happy ending.

Because mine is about to really, really suck.

Epilogue

Hendor, for all his faults, never asked questions. Piya Nahara appreciated that in him.

He said nothing, for example, when Piya ordered him to wait outside his ship for her return. He said nothing when she emerged a few minutes later from her childhood home, her hands stained blue and the wild light of generations of her mothers in her eyes. The cries from the compound meant nothing to him. Denavra nearly made it to his ship, screaming for his help; he watched Piya Nahara snap her neck like a bird's, raised an eyebrow, and went back to altering his consciousness.

"It's getting dark," was all he said when Piya finally rejoined him, wearing a sturdy set of pants and a jacket she'd stripped from one of the Pitonki bodies, a knapsack containing a few essentials slung over her shoulder.

Piya looked back at the compound building, which cast a reddish glow across the snow to Hendor's ship.

Fire raged from all three stories. The alien Lang had left just enough of her own strange sabotage behind in the power core to trigger an immensely satisfying explosion.

"Not so much," she said.

The wind whistled past the compound ruins. Ash swirled in the night air.

Innocence was not the same thing as knowing nothing.

Piya Nahara had never been innocent.

CPSIA information can be obtained
at www.ICGtesting.com
Printed in the USA
LVHW090719280621
691273LV00029B/346